Righteous
Maleficia
Emir Skalonja

RIGHTEOUS MALEFICIA
©2016 Emir Skalonja
Second Edition
All rights reserved
First edition published in 2015 by Emir Skalonja
Edited by Christina Hargis Smith
Proofread by Maura Atkinson Butler
Cover art by Jeffrey Kosh Graphics
Published by Optimus Maximus Publishing, LLC

ISBN-10: 1-944732-07-1
ISBN-13: 978-1-944732-07-3

DEDICATED

To my wife, Nicole, this spellbinding tome of wonders.

Acknowledgements

I grew up reading King, H.P. Lovecraft and Poe; I suppose these masters of the genre have shaped my ghastly vision when it comes to torture and perseverance of the human spirit. And I love writing about that. I love creating characters and putting them through trials and bloody adventures. I'm a visual person, though, and film is my first love and passion. As a filmmaker by nature, writing always came to me naturally, but only in the form of a screenplay.

And at times, films leave a lot to be desired, there has to be a lot of suspension of disbelief. So, as long as I can remember, I always wanted to write a novel. It was the need to tell a story, start to finish, without cuts, or fadeouts or time lapses.

But writing something as immense as a novel was intimidating to say the least. Over the past, well ten years or so, I had started numerous books of various genres, lengths, stories and such. Every single one met the same fate where I had just deleted the entire document.

Finally, I decided to write about something I like: history. But then, I needed a story. Well, I love all things that deal with witchcraft. Then, I decided to write about the oppression of people by the church in middle ages and those people turning to witchcraft.

Long story short, it was a tremendous ride and on that ride I was joined by many great people that made it all possible for me to happen.

First and foremost, I would like to thank my wife, Nicole. She has been with me from the very starts and made sure that I never gave up. She is my first proof reader and I run all my ideas and stories by her. I couldn't imagine this process without her by my side.

A very big and special thank you to my publisher Christina Hargis Smith, for never giving up on me; for pushing me constantly to better myself as a writer and to deliver an amazing end product. Honestly, the woman never gives up and constantly works with her writers to make sure everything goes the way it should. She is a trooper!

Thank you to all the beta readers for their time and much appreciated feedback. You made me see things differently, from another perspective.

Last but not least, a big thank you to Maura Atkinson Butler for her time with additional edits and proofreads and the last much needed peace of mind.

RIGHTEOUS MALEFICIA

A Novel by
Emir Skalonja

1

EMIR SKALONJA

PROLOGUE

Deep in the woods, on the outskirts of Blythe's hollow, villagers gathered around an old witch in hopes that she could ease their troubles. Such was human nature, to cling to thinnest of threads of hope if it meant the decision between life or death, no matter if the help was natural or supernatural. In the darkest of times, desperation drives people to explore options that were before deemed unthinkable.

The witch sat in her circle of bones made of all sorts, shapes, and sizes. There were numerous chalices meticulously placed just within her arm's reach. Each one of them was filled with different herbs and concoctions that served a purpose not entirely known to those that wanted help.

The night was still and silent, save for brief whimpers that would escape those weeping villagers that looked upon her ritual both with awe and hope. She sat there, paying them no mind, deep in her thoughts as she chanted slowly, quietly. She swayed back and forth, only occasionally glancing at the bodies laid out before her. She had seen her fair share of horrors throughout life, but as the time passed such travesties only became more grotesque and vile. People had become objects of most sinister evil anyone could ever imagine; they were the pawns of violence and torture only most morbid and disturbed minds could fathom. And as though sheer cruelty of humans was not enough, then came pestilence, the disease that they claimed was sent down from the Heavens because of the man's transgression against God.

It was just another punishment they said, divine this time around.

They had brought her a woman, and her little girl who was no more than six or seven years of age. Both were barely clothed and shivering as

3

if they had been stranded outside in a field during the middle of the winter.

It was the disease, the witch thought, still paying no mind to the people that gathered around her. The villagers had brought her the goods she needed from their lord's manor as a payment for her services. What little they brought was most likely stolen. She made good use of them and most of the time she would never see the villagers again. Perhaps it was that they feared for their lives because they went against the Church's teachings, or feared the punishment exacted by the cruel Lord Kenway, so they ran far away from the village and the cruelty that surrounded them.

Most likely it was that they were caught upon their return from her ritual and taken to the dungeons of the Church. She knew very well about those and what bloody murder was committed in them. The villagers told the tales of their friends being taken away by Kenway's guards or the priests, and how they were never seen again.

The witch focused her mind and energy back on the two people in front of her. The fever was cooking them alive, almost burning their flesh. Starting at the armpits and going further down their bodies, she could see the buboes, the sores that boiled large on the surface that had already burst open and spew out pus.

She reached out for the little dish by her side where she had mixed the herbs the villagers brought and rubbed the mixture on a cloth she took out from a boiling cauldron.

She rubbed the sores on the woman and the little girl with the medicinally infused rag as she chanted, slightly louder now, and swayed like a branch in the wind.

Smoke from the fire pit began to rise and spread its tendrils, engulfing the two bodies, and as it did, their shivering slowly subsided. The witch's chanting intensified as she spoke the old pagan words, words long ago forbidden by the Church. She waved her hand over the almost lifeless woman and child, feeling their waning energies and transferring some of hers into them.

Amidst the smoke and her chanting, the mother and child woke up suddenly, as if from a bad dream, and began to scream in confusion. The mother frantically examined the girl, grabbing her face into her hands,

4

brushing her hair aside from her sweaty forehead. She hugged her daughter as the villagers began to clap and cheer in excitement. Magically, the buboes began to dry out before their eyes, retreating and healing, scarring over like old wounds.

The witch stopped her chant and retreated back into the circle of skulls. Sitting with legs crossed and head lowered, she gazed at the ground, sighing in exhaustion. Flashing scenes of murder and grotesque torture began to creep into her head as the villagers started to surround her once again. In the vision, from a spectral plane of alternate existence, the witch stood amidst the chaos, her body levitating and merely observing the turmoil and bloodshed below her floating self. From this apparitional perspective, she could see innocent people as they died; they were all mutilated, one by one. Some were tortured for fun, some because they had sinned. *Sin, what a funny word*, the enchantress thought to herself. Suddenly she saw a strange man walking tall, striding through the village seemingly inured to all the destruction, against the murder and mayhem that was occurring in the witch's foresight. Though on a different astral plane, she could feel his strength and righteous aura coming through.

Perhaps the spirits were announcing an end to the troubled times, she thought in her trance, and end to the suffering and bloodshed. The omens were everywhere, one only needed to pay close attention when they presented themselves. Perhaps that's what the mysterious man was, an omen. Through the thick fog of the battlefield that the countryside had become, she tried to close in on his face and see into his eyes, for the eyes are a gateway into one's soul.

Her vision came to an abrupt end as one of the villagers placed his hand on her shoulder.

"Thank you, Magdalene," the man said and smiled at her. His dirty face was streaked by tears having been born of joy from the recent healing of his loved ones, or from anguish and despair from the travesties that had been occurring in the village. Magdalene was unsure of which.

She looked at him and said, "Let them leave this place, the village. It is for their own good. Take them far away."

The man looked back at her, knowing very well what she meant. He simply nodded and walked away with the rest of them.

"Far away," Magdalene said after them. "Far away."

CHAPTER ONE

Blythe's Hollow, England, 1392

The two priests strolled side by side through dimly lit halls of the church as the monotonous prayer of other monks echoed from the sanctuary above them. They descended further into the lower chambers, their footsteps in sync as they travelled. Hoods were drawn over their heads, covering just below their eyes and shrouding their faces with shadows.

They walked slowly, knowing that their task at hand had very little opportunity of fleeing elsewhere. There was a certain degree of contentness in their stride and their voices, a smugness that almost bordered the notion of extreme power and might.

"This is another one, isn't it? How many does that make now?" asked Father Johns, the taller and skinnier of the two.

The shorter one, Father Lawrence scoffed. "Who knows, dear Brother? They are herded in like the cattle they are. It seems as though the village has been rife with those dabbling in these horrific acts. We have continued to round them up as we discover their transgressions, and sadly, the numbers continue to rise."

"You do not say," Father Johns spoke back. "That many souls have been tainted, Father Lawrence?" the man asked with surprise that hinted at excitement.

"Yes, Brother. It has been a terrible discovery that so many of our flock have gone over to the dark side. Yet at the same time, it fills me with joy that we have saved just as many poor, lost souls. Granted, those that have been lost will pay the price for straying from the righteous path of our Lord and Savior. With our intervention and absolving of sins, they can make their journey to approach Heaven's gates with untainted souls."

"That is very true."

Father Lawrence crossed himself. The battle against sin was treacherous but it had to be won no matter what. No punishment was too severe for those who went against God or against the good book of their Lord.

Nothing was forbidden in the war against sin.

"The one that is in the chamber now was caught using the same herbal mix in an attempt to heal her sick mother. It is the exact combination that the others have used, we have confirmed this. Furthermore, all of them recite some devilish words as they administer this so called cure. It is pure blasphemy!"

"They are possessed," Father Johns said and scoffed at the ridiculousness of the entire situation. Men and women played witches and wizards in the village and as such, might as well have spit in the face of God. Who were they to try to take the matters in their own hands and go against God's will?

"The Devil is in our midst, Brother. Mind him very much so. He has taken a shape of someone in the village and he will stop at nothing to deceive us."

"Aye, these are troubled times," Father Johns said.

"Indeed they are."

They finally arrived at the lowest level of the church and continued the short distance to the heavy wooden door adorned with two rows of tiny spikes and bolts in the middle.

"What is her name?" Father Johns asked as he crossed himself.

"Edith. We have confiscated all of the herbal medicine she was using in her pathetic attempt to heal her mother. Now that woman has become another victim of this black magick and her soul must be cleansed too."

"Has she confessed?"

"Last I heard, she did. At least her soul is now saved and will not burn for an eternity."

"She still must pay for her transgression," Johns said then crossed himself again. He reached for the entry and gave it a forceful pull as its weight threatened to topple him off his feet. The heavy door creaked open slowly with his effort.

"That she will, Brother." Father Lawrence smiled under his hood.

The men entered the chamber; it was as dimly lit as the halls they had just walked through. The entire place smelled of old blood, sweat, and charred flesh. An iron maiden was placed in the far corner, across the room from the priests. The device stood there, its doors were open with pieces of skin and meat still hanging from the sharp points that lined its inside. A pool of drying blood was beneath the contraption. The entire room was filled with a sense of dread; if the walls had a voice, they would scream in agony. The villagers knew very well that whoever was brought to this forsaken place, they were as good as dead, as no one ever came back.

A few feet away from the iron maiden, from the ceiling hung two metal cages. These were rusty, with remnants of old bones from the previous victims whose fate had let them into this ominous room of death and carnage. In the center of the room was the rack, a contraption used to stretch a person and dislocate all of their joints and limbs. Next to this was the poor peasant woman Edith who had been the culprit of the latest accusations of witchcraft. Edith looked to be no more than twenty years old and was a pretty girl by many standards despite her numerous cuts and bruises, though that beauty was now blemished and tortured, dragged through hell and back. The young maiden now wished to die, wanted this ordeal to be over and done with so she could embark upon a new journey away from this horrendous suffering.

Edith hung in a contraption that was positioned to the right of the dark, cavernous room. She was naked, positioned upside down, with her legs pulled apart with two thick, tight ropes. Her hands were also bound and spread. Curiously she resembled an upside down star. Blood dripped from the wounds that she received during earlier torture sessions prior to being fastened to the device in which she was currently encumbered.

The girlish energy she always had was long gone; she was thirsty, tired, and in severe pain, only wanting this to end. The words that tried to escape her mouth became lodged in her throat so no sound would come out. The men surrounding her were only a blur as her vision deteriorated from the constant hits to her head and the severe swelling that reduced her eyes to mere slits.

Her life was seeping out, leaving barely a shell.

There were no more traces of the pretty young girl who enjoyed life to the fullest. Edith had loved her mother and God, who had now forsaken her and left her at the mercy of these cruel men. *Who were these men who held themselves so high up, nearly elevating themselves to the level of God himself?*

"So this is she," Father Johns said in observation. "Such a shame. The Devil knows no boundaries. None of us are safe from the cold embrace of temptation and straying from the path that was set forth for us by the Almighty."

A sickly looking monk approached the two priests. His face was pale and bony, splattered with dry patches of blood from the past victims. He cowered in front of the two. "Father Johns. Father Lawrence. Do you wish to proceed? She has confessed all of her sins so I do believe it is time."

Father Lawrence approached and examined the girl. He had to crouch as she hung upside down, her arms and legs tautly splayed. He closed his eyes and said a prayer, and blessed the girl by drawing the shape of a cross on her forehead.

"I nomine patri et fili spiritu sancte," Father Lawrence whispered the words and nodded his head. He rose, he nodded to the other priests as he held his cross. "Brother Samuel, she is ready. God have mercy on her soul."

The pallid monk crossed himself and waved at a bulkier man who was standing by a table with numerous tools laid out on it. He was the executioner and wore a hood that covered his entire head, save for the two eye holes. He acknowledged the order and lifted a large, long saw that had a handle on each end.

The two priests stepped back a few paces, retreating to the other side of the room near the door to make room for what was to come.

The executioner walked behind Edith and extended the saw through her spread legs to Samuel who stood on the other side of her. He took it with eagerness, a smile lightly playing on his lips. The two men positioned the filthy blade in between Edith's legs, letting its teeth nestle against her womanly folds. The terrified young maiden again began to moan and cry. Tears mixed with blood and dirt ran down her face and onto the floor beneath her head.

"Please...stop. I beg of you. Stop...," she managed to utter through a swollen throat.

Samuel looked back at the two priests who nodded in unison.

The executioner grunted; though from the sound of it, one could infer his smile spreading under his hood as he seemed to enjoy his work.

They began to pull back and forth, lightly at first until their efforts intensified in both motion and power. Edith screamed just as the blade began to rip into her flesh, then she fell into shock and her sounds immediately ceased, her voice was stolen by the pain. They notched the woman, breaking through the bones of her pelvis then continuing unhindered through her lower bowels and stomach until the blade was almost in between her breasts. Edith's rib bones cracked, her skin tore like paper and her vital organs fell out and sloshed juicily on the floor at the men's feet. Her body had been methodically and brutally sawed in half by the murderers employed by the Church.

The already pale Samuel was winded and panting from the expended energy, yet he also seemed to have found a pleasurable release in his efforts at bisecting the young peasant girl. He licked his lips and looked down at the innards that skidded across the floor with every movement of his feet. Something else was aroused in him as he watched the two halves of Edith's body, held together only by her head, finally fall to each side and then slide around in the pool of her own blood and intestines, when the ropes holding her feet were finally loosened. He thought of her beauty before she was beaten beyond recognition. If he only thought of it sooner, he would have had his way with her, oh yes, he would. It was justifiable as he was sure that a girl like she had been whoring around the village.

Fathers Lawrence and Johns crossed themselves as the young lady's body came apart in two pieces.

"And another leaves this world prematurely," Father Johns said.

"You speak the truth. Though it pains me to see so many of our congregation die. It also does my heart good to know that we have stopped some of the evil from further spreading through our home of Blythe's Hollow."

"Are there any more coming today?" Samuel asked as the executioner began to pick up the young maiden's guts, placing them onto a large tray and carry them to the hearth. They sizzled in the fire as he tossed them in.

"I am afraid so," Father Lawrence answered without turning. "The sinners never rest. It will do us great good if we keep that in our minds."

"Well, alright then. We shall clean this mess and wait for more." Samuel turned his head like a mad man between the two priests and his helper, who was still cleaning up the remains of poor Edith. He seemed blood thirsty, like a rabid animal, eagerly anticipating his next victim. One could only imagine the enjoyment he received from killing. His eyes spoke of such gratification.

"Please, Brother Samuel. Do that for us, will you not?" Father Johns asked as he smiled at the man.

"Oh yes I will, Father Johns. I am here to serve the Lord."

The priest turned to join Father Lawrence who was already waiting in the hallway. He exited and shut the heavy wooden door, leaving the two torturers behind and sealing in the evidence of the ongoing massacre.

Samuel took the broom that was leaning against the wall and began sweeping the remnants of skin and bone that his assistant had missed. He mumbled as he did so, saying prayers for the girl whose remains were currently being licked by the flames, incinerated and cleansed by the holy fire.

Father Lawrence returned to his room after he had parted ways with Father Johns. It had only been a little past one o'clock in the afternoon but he felt as if the day had been dragging on forever. Serving the Lord and punishing the wicked took a toll on a man.

It seemed to be a never ending battle to Father Lawrence. It felt as if no matter what he did, no matter how much he preached and provided guidance, the sinners were somehow always a step ahead of him and going against God. Despite his efforts, there were many that disobeyed the good book and blasphemed. Each time someone would transgress, he felt as if they were going against him. It had become personal and he believed that the war had to be fought on that level.

He wasn't the young man he once was, no longer that fifteen year old, bright boy who was full of vigor that had entered the monastery and chosen the life of piety in obedience to God. That was forty some years ago and throughout his servitude, he had seen a great deal of wickedness and transgression against the church and God. Many times he had come face to face with the Devil and had always come out triumphant. These devils did not have horns and tails. Each and every time the fiend had disguised himself as either a man or a woman of an ordinary stature. Father James Lawrence could see through the beast's trickery though. He could not be fooled. When the plague had come to the British Isles about a year ago and entered Blythe's Hollow, everything seemed to change. The peasants went into frenzy and it was not too long before they started dabbling in witchcraft. Older women in the village started mixing strange herbal remedies in an attempt to cure the pestilence.

That is what it was, witchcraft. Father Lawrence was sure of it. The Bubonic Plague was a punishment, a test sent by God himself. It was a punishment for all the sin that was infecting the population. And then, at the same time, it was a test to show who the worthy ones were. So far, he had been very saddened by the outcome.

A knock came on his door startling him from his deep thoughts. He hesitated for a moment and then spoke. "Come," Father Lawrence said and sighed.

"Father Lawrence?" came the voice before a younger priest revealed himself. It was Father Francis Williams. "Do you have a moment?"

"Yes, dear Francis. What is the matter?" asked Father Lawrence as he began to lower his body on the bed. "From the sound of your voice, it seems that you are troubled."

The young man's eyes wandered around the room with uncertainty. "Well, Father, I wish I could bring you some better news but, it looks like we have some more people that were just brought in from the village."

"And?"

"They were caught by Lord Kenway's men who said they were stealing from his storage. They are in very bad shape. They have been beaten by the looks of it," Francis said, some resentment in his voice, though he did attempt to cover it up.

Father Lawrence sighed again. "Rightfully so, my young Father, rightfully so. Have you forgotten 'thou shall not steal'?" His voice was

13

stern yet understanding. Father Williams was young and inexperienced, led by his heart most of the time. Sin had to be judged swiftly and severely as far as the elder priest was concerned.

"No, Father, I have not, though I do believe these severe beatings are uncalled for."

"Have them put in the cell and wait there," Father Lawrence dismissed and closed his eyes. "That is all."

Father Williams understood this to be the signal to leave Father Lawrence to his privacy. "Yes, Father," he said and left.

CHAPTER TWO

The day was brutally hot. Edgar took a break from the tedious and grueling task of wood cutting. He looked up to the sky to see that there was not a single cloud floating about. The sun was slightly beyond its highest point; it was just past one o'clock by Edgar's estimation. The July sun shone bright on the village and it just may be one of the hottest days they had thus far. It was as if the gates of Hell had opened up.

Edgar tossed his axe aside, burying the blade in the dirt, and then took his shirt off, tying it around his waist. Sweat dripped down his sore body in rivers. The drenched arm he used to wipe his forehead did nothing more than smear the accumulating dirt there. His arms ached and still vibrated from constantly swinging the axe and the repeated impact it made with wood. It was only recently that he was pulled from farming duty when Lord Drake Kenway decided to add another extension to his already expansive manor and now required more timber to be chopped down for the build.

Edgar wondered what the old lunatic had in mind. The manor was already so big that he imagined it to be a dizzying maze inside. He had only seen the courtyard and the front entrance to the estate. Yet he imagined the quarters and corridors to be vast and confusing. He would often sit with Farah on the hill just outside Blythe's Hollow where the woods started, and look upon the village from there. From this perspective they would see Lord Kenway's vast estate in its entirety and speculate how everything looked inside and just what went on in there. Edgar imagined that if the life was so miserable on the outside, the life on the inside of the manor was worse tenfold, considering how cruel and relentless Kenway could be to the villagers.

Edgar dropped to the ground in exhaustion, taking a seat next to his worn axe. He did not really care if anyone had seen him take a break. The guards had been gone for at least an hour. They most likely fled the heat in search of cool shelter and some cold water, as was the case with all the privileged few. These privilege ones were mainly guards, the clergy, and anyone else that might be residing in the manor, which were mainly Kenway's relatives. However, there were others around who had noticed his lack of work, though at this moment Edgar could not be concerned.

"You know, you are lucky Kenway's watch dogs are not here, otherwise it would be you in the dirt instead of that axe." A man came behind him, grabbing Edgar's shoulders and shaking him. Then the man laughed and sat next to Edgar. "I would hate to see you like that, friend. Tis a rotten way to end your life, you know that. One day you are walking on the dirt, the next you are in it. That is just how the life comes and goes these days."

"You have always been the funny man of the whole crowd around here, Bradyn," Edgar said and could not help but smile. After all, he was somewhat startled by his best friend. The truth was that if one of Kenway's men saw him, he would have been severely beaten. The Lord ruled his dominion with an iron fist and allowed no one under his command to be laggard or derelict in their duty. Punishment was swift and often. Kenway and his guards were brutal, without regard for the lives of those in his servitude.

"But I always come in the time of need, my friend," Bradyn said as he reached for his waist where a lambskin pouch filled with water hung. He untied it and handed it to Edgar. The water sloshing inside made Edgar salivate with anticipation of his tongue being whetted by the simple elixir. When he touched the pouch, he could feel the coldness of the water inside. He was grateful that there was plenty of it left and his good friend was willing to share the wealth. He uncapped the pouch and drank until he almost gagged.

"Will's daughter brought two of them. The other men breaking the stones kept one for themselves. I think one of them passed out earlier from the heat. At least that is what they said."

"It does not surprise me," Edgar replied as he wiped his mouth. He then coughed to get the extra water that choked him out of his throat. "It has been hot, no doubt about it."

"It has been hellish. I take it that description does it better justice. Who let Satan up here with his fire and heat?" Bradyn asked as he took the water from Edgar and indulged in some much needed refreshment. Then he thought just how loud he spoke that name, *Satan*, and briefly looked around to make sure that it raised no suspicion. You could not be more careful out in the open where everyone heard you and even the houses and trees had ears. At least it seemed that way.

They sat in silence, Edgar leaned back and propped himself on his elbows. He tilted his head back and his eyes gazed over the perfectly blue sky. He felt Bradyn's eyes studying him and when he turned to look at his friend, he was greeted with a concerned look.

"What?" Edgar asked and raised one of his eyebrows.

"They took James and Raymond," Bradyn uttered softly, sounding distant, his voice almost a whisper.

"Who took them? What are you talking about?" Edgar now sat up straight. Then he realized what Bradyn meant. He now had a look of uneasiness too. James and Raymond were decent, hardworking men, though at times they had a bad habit of questioning and talking back to the authority. They had never done anything as severe to warrant being 'taken' away. Being taken meant that Lord Kenway turned over his prisoners and let the church deal with a particular problem. These problems were more often than not religious in nature. Lately very few people ever returned from the church.

"They were caught stealing earlier today. They were found in the man's storage, going through the stuff and all. It was discovered after inventory was taken that food had been missing for the last few weeks. Now they have assumed that it had been James and Raymond stealing all along," Bradyn said. He picked up a piece of hay and put it in his mouth to chew. It hung on his lip as he turned it about with his tongue. He was nervous, Edgar could tell.

"Can you blame them?" Edgar asked as he looked away out in the field. "We slave all day and get to fight over crumbs to feed ourselves. That is all we receive for the hard labor we endure. It is a life not fit for an animal!" He grew frustrated and it began to show through his tired exterior. He looked down at his stomach which was growling in hunger. Edgar was never a large or bulky man but he noticed that he had begun to lose a considerable amount of weight. He then lifted his gaze back up again and continued to look over the field and the mounds of hay.

"I know," Bradyn almost whispered so no one else would hear, "but we cannot just go around stealing. You know how Kenway is. He has killed for less." He nervously looked around and was relieved to notice that the other laborers who had been chopping wood nearby paid them no attention.

"And now the church is doing the same thing. It looks to me that they have actually overtaken the job of punishing us, from Kenway, that is," Edgar said.

"It is true and terrifying. I am afraid to look at someone the wrong way. I am fearful I might end up in one of those dungeon chambers in the church. That is why I said we need to be careful and not do anything stupid. These are hard times, with plague upon us and all." Bradyn continued to look around nervously in fear because if the wrong person overheard certain conversations, one could be severely punished.

"Indeed they are," Edgar said and finally got back up. He took the axe from the dirt and walked to the pile of logs.

Bradyn followed close behind, carrying his own axe. The men began to chop the logs in silence. Edgar pondered the conversation he had thus far with his friend as he labored. Bradyn was right; Kenway and his hounds and the church were looking to put anyone in a cell for whatever ridiculous reason they found fitting. People were scared and suspicious, even of each other.

Two years ago, Blythe's Hollow was a quiet little village with no more than a bandit or two passing by. Though the times had always been rough for peasant families such as Edgar's and Bradyn's, at least back then they never feared for their lives, to the extent that they did now.

When the plague came to the village some months ago, everything changed for the worse. People died every single day from the pestilence. Those that suffered and turned to certain unconventional methods in an attempt to cure the disease were accused by the Church as partaking in witchcraft and were given a swift and severe punishment.

Two months ago, George, a man Edgar knew, that worked in the kitchen of Kenway's manor, had stolen some herbs from the storage and took them to a woman that lived just outside the village. She was old, but just how old she actually was, Edgar could not say. Someone had mentioned once that she was well into her nineties. She lived by herself deep in the woods and he was sure she had an extensive underground passageway that would help her escape and avoid Kenway's men when they were sent to retrieve her. But something in Edgar's mind nudged the idea that the old woman could not possibly work on her own. He had seen her once, from a distance, and by the looks of her, he had been surprised she was still alive.

The woman was very well known for preserving the old pagan ways; the herbs that people would bring her- it was usually a very specific list- she would use to make her potions through a series of rituals. These rituals, so the people claimed, invoked the spirits and the presence from a world not of our own. Due to such practices, the church had instantly labeled her a witch and there was a constant hunt for her. What Edgar found interesting, and he was sure many other people who had gone to her did as well, was the fact that neither the church, nor Kenway's men could track her down. It was rather comical, he thought.

George was one of those who had sought her help after his oldest son had come down with the plague. However, George was quickly taken away. Edgar was sure there was someone who had been watching the villagers and reporting their doings to either Kenway or the monks in the church. Bradyn was right, he told himself once more as he began to swing the axe and cut the wood.

"So do you think they will come out alive? Do you think the priests will let them go?" Bradyn asked as he began to chop his own stack of wood.

Edgar had been shrouded in his thoughts since they had resumed working after their break. Bradyn's voice jolted him back to reality. Edgar became aware of the surroundings and heard the splitting of timber and the field stones being stacked on carts by other men. "To be honest with you, I really do not know," Edgar finally said, "I hate to say it, and though it pains and angers me, I think it is the end of them."

"Do you really think so?" Bradyn asked, his voice almost childish, imploring Edgar to give him some hope. James and Raymond were good, hard working men who got caught trying to help their families. Mere thoughts of them being killed for something like that destroyed Bradyn on the inside. Hell, he had known James since childhood. To Bradyn it seemed unfair that good people, who were just trying to aid their families and survive, were dragged into the bowels of Hell by the priests.

"I sure hope so, Bradyn, I really do. But as you see, we are on a rather short supply of hope these days. It has slowly been going from bad to worse and what else can we expect,

I simply do not know. I wouldn't want to say anything that would give you false hope. It kills a man further. It delivers a final blow."

"God help us all," Bradyn said and crossed himself.

"I just hope He hears our prayers," Edgar said and fell silent once more. He looked like he was about to say something else but cut himself short.

"What is it?" Bradyn asked.

Edgar hesitated for a moment and decided not to answer.

"What is it, Edgar?" Bradyn asked again. "Do not keep anything from me, you hear. I need to know what goes on in that thick skull of yours."

Edgar smiled at the remark but the simper disappeared quickly.

"Do not think you will tease me with your hidden thoughts and then just send me on my merry way, my friend. There are plenty of secrets around here as it is. And who are we but simple, filthy peasants in the eyes of the few that hold the power over us? The likes of us stick together. It is the only way to have any chance of survival. So please, tell me what is on your mind."

"It is something I thought of just now, Bradyn. Why is it that God is not answering our prayers? Why is it that He has put men in charge who murder us faster than the plague itself? I ask God this every night and wait for a sign, an answer, something…"

"Faith is the only thing we have left, Edgar. Faith in God and that He has a plan for all of us. Let us only hope the plan does not involve us ending up in those bloody dungeons."

"And here you go again with the talks of hope. Will you stop that?" Edgar said, somewhat sarcastically. "Talking of hope makes me believe there is some left. I do not want to lie to myself."

"Well at least have some for me. Or even better yet, have some for Farah. You would hope for the best for her at least, wouldn't you?"

"I guess you are right." Edgar said and gave his friend a quick smile. "How is it that you do this?"

"Do what?"

"Make me smile with your banter. I am telling you, you have some art in your trickery to control human emotions." Edgar now let out a laugh. "Maybe I should send you over to Kenway and have them all swayed to our will." He then laughed again.

"No, I think I will pass on that. I only do it for friends," Bradyn said and smiled himself.

CHAPTER THREE

The house that Edgar lived in with his wife Farah and his elderly, nearly crippled, father Cederic, was barely fit for a human being. It was small, crudely made, and looked like it had seen better days. The seasons have definitely left their mark on the façade and it now served solely as a shelter from the outside world and nothing more. Each time Edgar would come back home from his long days out in the field, the appearance of the shanty would remind him of their dire situation.

It was not just him and Farah that had it bad; one could look at the entire village and see the despair and misery. His was not the only home that was crumbling. There were plenty of houses, if they could even be called that, in the village with both makeshift roofs and uneven walls that were home to families of five or six or even more. One could easily get away with calling them hovels instead of homes and they were the complete opposite of the grandeur of Lord Kenway's manor.

No matter how bad the things get, Farah had always told him, there was always someone worse off than them. Edgar tried to appreciate that comment but only to a certain extent. Enough was enough, and tolerating this rotten way of living was accepting one's defeat.

He stood there for a moment and looked at the house. At least the day was nice enough to chase away some of the gloominess that was on his mind. He hesitated going in there, all dirty and stinking of grass and sweat. He had to tell Farah that Lord Kenway's guards had captured James and Raymond for thievery and had handed them over to the Church for punishment. He was sure that the two men were most likely not coming back alive. At least once, he wished to return home and give Farah some good news. It did not even have to be good for that matter, provided that it was not bleak and morbid as always.

Edgar saw Farah in the window watching for his return home. She opened the door and came out and greeted him with kiss and a warm embrace. "How was your day, love?" she asked and snuck her arm under his as they walked inside.

Edgar shrugged, sighed, and scoffed, all in that order, all in an effort not to answer. "Tiring," he said at last as he sat down. "Very tiring, indeed."

His father, Cederic was in bed in a very small room, with the door slightly ajar. "How is he?" Edgar asked.

"Just about the same. There really has been no change, which is good I suppose. He could be a lot worse. We have to be grateful for that, at least"

Farah then took out two bowls and walked to a cauldron that hung over a hearth that was covered in ash. The fire had been put out a long time ago and whatever she had been cooking was already done and ready to be eaten. It was a stew of some sort. She filled one bowl and placed it on the table in front of Edgar who started eating immediately. The wooden spoon with which he ate seemed to not be big enough to quickly satisfy the hunger Edgar had. He ate as if he had been starving for weeks, which, essentially he had been. They all had.

Farah watched him for a moment, then placed her hand on his shoulder briefly and walked away to fill herself a bowl. When she did, she came back and sat opposite him.

"You were in the field today? Chopping wood again?"

Edgar nodded in answer.

"I cannot believe what Kenway is having you do," she said as she began to eat, and thought of the manor.

"Neither can the other men. People are starving and he's building himself a bigger house," Edgar said without looking up. "Imagine the logic in that." He continued to eat greedily. He then paused for a moment to half look up at Farah and saw her looking at him, her spoon waiting in the bowl. She smiled at him, warm and loving in an otherwise bleak and dreary existence. She was the only bright spot in the miserable life he woke up to every single day.

She took care of his father, who Edgar sometimes wished were already dead, so the old man would not suffer anymore. It was a horrible thought but Edgar could no longer bear witness to his always selfless and giving father deteriorate and endure any more pain in this world that was almost no longer worth living in.

He smiled back and continued to eat. That made him feel a little better, eased some stress, and for a moment, made him forget the outside world. But it did not take long for the thoughts of his day from earlier to come back knocking on his mind. He stopped eating once again and pondered his thoughts. Then he broke the silence. "Kenway's men took James and Raymond," he said coldly.

"What?" Farah asked, once again resting her spoon in the bowl. "What do you mean took them?"

"They were caught stealing from his storage. That is what Bradyn told me. He said the guards took them to the church. Who knows what is going to happen to them." He finished eating and pushed the bowl aside. He was still hungry but didn't say anything because he knew there wasn't enough food to go around.

"Oh dear Lord, that is terrible!" Farah said and crossed herself. It looked almost unnatural; her movement was absent, not her own. Perhaps there was no more passion in it, nothing but empty hope that things would look up and the two men would come back to the village alive. Yes, Edgar thought, there was no passion in Farah crossing herself. Her expression was almost blank when she did it. However, her concern for the two men was genuine, he could see that much. She was still a very loving woman, caring and always with a worry for his wellbeing, but over the past months she had developed such a cold exterior that on occasion she had appeared to be a completely different woman. Perhaps it was a natural mechanism of protection against everything the world managed to throw at them.

"Yes," Edgar said and looked at the room where his father slept. "But what are we to expect?"

"Not much I suppose," Farah answered, almost submissively. "People are starving. Everyone does what they must to survive, even if it is against the Lord's word."

Edgar thought about that for a moment, what Farah said. 'Lord's word,' the sentence echoed in his mind. He wasn't sure that was even a real thing anymore. There was so much death surrounding them that he wondered if this really was what God had intended for humanity.

"It is our basic instinct," Farah continued, "as humans, flawed as we are. We do what we deem necessary to preserve our life. I am sure James and Raymond did just that."

Edgar looked at his wife oddly, almost marveling at her words. She spoke softly and eloquently, almost as if she had been some educated nobility instead of a simple peasant's wife. But her words, no matter how out of place they appeared to be in their household, sounded truthful.

"That we do," Edgar said and nodded. Farah pushed her bowl aside and walked over to her husband. She hugged him from behind and kissed his cheek. He liked that very much. It was soothing.

"There is terrible evil out there, my love," Edgar said and gazed into nothingness. "When I am out working, I think of you and coming home to you and if that is something I did not have, I would question my very existence. Now I can only imagine what it must be like for James and Raymond's families."

"It must be terrifying," Farah agreed.

They stayed there like that for a little while. They were silent, each lost deep in their own thoughts. Just the company of one other was enough.

Eventually Edgar stood back up and returned the hug. Farah was a woman of a small stature by any standards, her head coming only to Edgar's chest. She rested her lovely face there and closed her eyes for a moment. Edgar kissed her forehead and then the two separated.

He walked over to the room where Cederic slept. Edgar peeked in and observed the old man for a moment. He slept peacefully at least, Edgar thought. He could provide his
beloved father with at least that much comfort.

"I fed him before you returned," said Farah as she cleaned up the bowls. "He ate a few spoonfuls and had some water. That is all I've managed."

"That is alright. He is better off sleeping. At least he is in peace for the moment."

Cederic looked older than he actually was. He was a man of fifty-five but looked to be well into the seventies. Malnutrition and heavy labor for many years had taken a toll on him and now he could barely move. Once a day, Edgar managed to take the debilitated man outside and help him move about. Now that the plague ravaged the cities as well as the countryside, those trips outside the house became less frequent as it was not worth the risk. Not only had the pestilence begun to sweep through the people of the village, it also affected the livestock. Nowhere was safe anymore. They could not hide from the devastation of the disease, nor from the abuse of their fellow man.

"I just wish there was something more I could do for him," Edgar said and sighed. "I hate seeing him like this. Sometimes I wonder if he would not be better off dead." He hated thinking about that, but at times, he could not help it. He truly wondered if his father would be better off resting in permanent peace, rather than in the condition he was now.

"I wish I could tell you, my love," Farah's voice came from the other room.

Edgar walked into this father's room, and placed his hand on the Cederic's forehead. "He is burning up with fever," Edgar said to Farah.

"I shall put a wet cloth on his head. It will cool him off a bit. It is scorching outside, I am surprised this entire village is not ablaze."

Within the next few minutes, she brought in a dish filled with water and had an old rag hanging off her shoulder. She dipped the cloth into the water and let it soak. She drained it, folded it, and then placed it on her father in law's forehead. The man groaned softly in his sleep.

"It is soothing," Farah said. "I bet it feels good on his head, a welcome relief to this torturous heat."

"Thank you," Edgar said as he placed his hand on her shoulder, and then walked away. He trudged outside and sat on the ground in front of the dilapidated shanty. He looked out over the hill where there were no houses to block the view. The sun had begun to set. Another day passed on Earth, that to him, felt more like purgatory. If this was God's test, he wasn't sure if he was passing or failing.

As he watched the sunset, he wondered how come God had put such evil men in charge over the people who so desperately needed His help. He felt like calling out to Him, yet restrained himself. It had not worked so far. Edgar felt as though he was drowning in the despair of the climate, from both the weather and of the current conditions of Blythe's Hollow and its very grave situation.

CHAPTER FOUR

A new day dawned, much darker than the one before. Black, ominous clouds loomed over Blythe's Hollow, so low in the sky that one might think that the village would get swallowed into the heavens.

Rain poured and washed the dirt from the previous day; it soaked the dry patches of land and made the trees and meadows lush green and full with color. Yet whatever color was there, whatever natural aura had tried to break its way through gloominess, the clouds were there to swallow it up.

The village looked dead, abandoned, and devoid of any signs of life as no one was moving about. A traveler venturing through the outskirts might have mistaken the village for some abandoned, forsaken ghost town that would best be avoided.

The heavy rain that washed the ever present heat had caked the paths in mud, some of it running down into the creek nearby and clouding it brown. The rooster that had been up for some time had screeched his song several times to mark the beginning of the new day but so far, no villagers had shown their faces. The animal let loose one final time and then fell silent. It was soaking wet, its feathers glistening in reflection of the thick drops of rain. It looked pathetic, beaten, and had seen better days. The hens sat there still and looking haggard with dead eyes. In this dim light and wetness, they all looked as though they had undergone some sort of demonic possession.

After the last screech of the rooster, and a deathly moment of silence in the entire village, the doors began to open on the houses and first signs of life began to appear. As they walked out of their homes, some of the peasants looked up to the sky with smiles on their faces, rain drops washing them clean from a certain degree of pain and misery.

The ground was soaking wet which was beneficial for the soil. The heat had scorched the plentiful crops and the season, many of the villagers thought, was lost. However, the rain was a welcome guest to those who worked the fields and relied on the crop to feed their families, even though the food that they grew was Lord Kenway's. Still, if there was no food in Kenway's household, the entire village was doomed.

People poured out of their homes, some carrying sacks, other carrying their tools to chop, plow, and sow. Those that had been making their way towards their work assignments now slowed down and started to gather near the church. The church was located on a slight hill east of the manor and looked down on the village as if from the heavens. Edgar always joked that it had been built on an elevated ground to make it be closer to God, when in reality, he said, they had put it up like that to defend from any possible riots from down trodden peasants.

The villagers slowed down, one by one, until they came to a complete stop. Almost in unison, they tilted their heads upward and looked at the church, or more precisely, what was in church's courtyard. Some looked on in disbelief, placing their hands over their mouths or their eyes, some quickly looked away, unable to bear witness to the horror before them.

Edgar had made his way toward the church along with everyone else. He could not see very clearly from his house what was in the courtyard, but the blurry silhouette of the scene did not leave much room for his imagination. He feared he knew what it was, yet still hoped to prove his mind wrong when he got closer. Knowing deep down that his worst fears would be answered, he had told Farah to stay inside and not come out until his return. Now he stood among the mass of thirty or forty villagers who had been on their way to work, now all staring up at the ghastly scene.

In the center courtyard, on the makeshift gallows, hung the naked, scarred, and bloody James and Raymond swaying in the wind. The rain was pelting their wounds, washing the blood from their ravaged and tortured bodies. Since their deaths were so recent, they still bled from their freshest wounds. Their life blood trickled down under them, onto the wooden platform, painting it red.

There was a murmur of disbelief from the crowd. The villagers were all distressed yet there was no surprise at the brutality of the deaths of the peasant men. No one, at least to Edgar's knowledge, expected the men to survive being taken away. What shocked everyone were the new, creative, and violent ways that the church was coming up with to punish the villagers. The torture practices were morbid and depraved and many wondered if this is what God really had in store for the rest of them, or if this were just a horrid and terrible nightmare.

Two hooded monks stood next to the gallows. Their faces were hidden away from the villagers. The large, arched church doors opened and the head priest Father Lawrence came out. He was followed by Father Johns and several other monks who rarely ventured out. They were the ones who generally performed all the tortures and executions that were ordered by Father Lawrence and Father Johns.

The soft murmur of the crowd subsided as Father Lawrence raised his arms to greet them. He was robed like the other monks but his and Father John' appeared to be more lavish; bright red cloth accented with darker, richer red stripes on the side. They wore gold necklaces that were adorned with fine chiseled crosses that hung down on their chests.

While the peasant people died trying to make their ends meet, where life was just one big fight for survival, Edgar thought, *these men flaunted their riches. Yet they were the ones who took the oath of piety.*

Father Lawrence stood in front of the two dangling corpses. Father Johns was poised just behind him and looked down at the crowd. Kenway's guards were there too, just in case something went wrong.

"Brothers and sisters," Father Lawrence began, his voice trying to raise itself over the pelting sound of rain and succeeding. It still carried powerfully, managing to reach even those standing in the back.

"It is with great sadness that I see the events in this village unfold before me," he continued. "As of late, it has come to my attention that with the plague upon us, some of you have given yourself to practices which are not allowed by our Holy Church. Not only are these unholy practices, but they are the ones that will banish you from the Heavenly gates for all eternity. I am speaking to you about black magick." He paused to take in the reaction of the people in the crowd.

"Yes, black magick," he said as he crossed himself. "It pains me to see our village brought so low by these ancient, pagan practices. It is all the work of the Devil himself. It is the Devil that is corrupting your minds and clouding your judgment. I ask of you to tell him *no* and keep our Lord and Savior in your heart. Only with His name on your lips and with the good book in your hand will you ward off evil and these dark forces that are on our doorstep."

He stopped, coughed, and then pointed at the two hanging bodies. "These men have succumbed to the dark forces. They have given their lives over to the Devil and have listened to his commands. They have stolen property that was not theirs! We have uncovered, with the help of our God's hand, that these men were connected to a heinous web of practitioners of this black magick!" He paused again to let his words sink in. To have the villagers watch two of their friends, naked and butchered, sway in the wind. To have them see what fate awaits those who go against God and His church.

"You aim to cure the plague; this pestilence which God has sent to punish us for our sins. You aim to go against His wish, against His word. Well, this is the fate that awaits you, brothers and sisters, if you give yourself over to the Devil. It is God's will for some of us to perish in this plague and it cannot be stopped. It cannot be undone. Hell awaits you if you go against his wish."

"We are already in Hell!" a voice came from someone in the crowd. Edgar couldn't see who the man was, but he thought him to be stupid for speaking out in defiance at such a public gathering. He might as well go ahead and surrender himself to either Kenway or the church. Edgar saw that Father Lawrence had caught a glimpse of the man that spoke out.

"Do not let yourself be swayed by the likes of them, the demons and heathens. They will be your doom!" Father Lawrence spoke more intensely now, with even more conviction. His face was red with anger, his eyes piercing every single soul in the crowd. "For this is the fate that awaits you when you stray away from God's grace."

He pointed at the bodies again, turned around and stopped to whisper something to Father Johns. Then the priests walked back into the church, followed by the monks.

The crowd began to disperse, overlapping voices mixed in with the sound of rain hitting the now soaked, swampy paths. Footsteps sloshed away from the courtyard. Edgar remained behind, staring at the church and the dangling, mutilated bodies of the two men he had known for a very long time. Edgar no longer had any tears left to mourn the men…or any other of the dozens that had fallen victim to the priests and their supposed teachings of the righteous way to attain salvation.

Edgar started to turn when a voice called out to him.

"Edgar," came the voice behind him. It was Bradyn. He had been somewhere in the crowd when the sermon was happening and the expression on his face looked much liked Edgar's; filled with anger and misery.

"That was terrible. I mean, *is* terrible. How could they do this?" He shook his head in disbelief, eyes traveling from Edgar to the bodies and then back to Edgar. The guards were still there, lingering around. They watched as the villagers dispersed then left toward Kenway's manor.

Edgar grabbed Bradyn by the shoulder and pushed him onward. "Let us go," he said and hurried his friend. "There is no reason to stick around."

"We have to get their bodies, Edgar. We cannot just leave them like that!" Bradyn protested and tried to go back but could not make it past Edgar who had a firm grip on him.

"That is not a good idea. Trust me."

"For the love of God, we cannot leave them like that. Those are our friends over there, hanging like some dogs," Bradyn continued, his teeth and fists clenched. Edgar had always known Bradyn to be a meek individual, non-confrontational to others. His friend had changed before his eyes and if Edgar didn't stop him, it would mean a death sentence for both of them.

"They *were* our friends. Those are just their bodies hanging there. Turn around and go! You will get us both killed if you continue and the guards take notice of us!" Edgar shoved him once more to get him to move along.

Bradyn eased off a little. He calmed himself, turned and walked ahead of Edgar. "You know it is not right. Us leaving them like this and all. What kind of people are we if we leave our friends like that? Can you tell me that, Edgar? Can you?" He spoke more calmly, collecting himself as they walked. "I mean they are leaving them like that, like they are nothing, with no proper burial."

"I understand," Edgar finally said. "But they are just waiting for us to get up there so we can become their next victims. Unfortunately, the only thing we can do right now is keep our heads down. The less attention we attract, the better."

"This is wrong, Edgar," Bradyn said and shook his head. Most of the villagers were well ahead of them, only some still passing them by. They all slowly made their ways to their assigned positions, heads down, shoulders slouched and defeated.

"I know it is," Edgar agreed and sighed.

It rained for the remainder of the day.

CHAPTER FIVE

The room was dimly lit; the only source of light was a candle burning on the wall by the door and the fire crackling lightly in the fireplace. The meager flames painted the stone walls with wavering, weak light that cast shadows so deep and frightening that one could see them as a monster coming to life before his very eyes.

There was a simple cross placed just above the mantel, a table holding a bible sat next to the hearth. There were two chairs, cushioned for comfort, which sat in front of the fireplace; these Father Lawrence used to entertain his guests. This was not to say that Father Lawrence had many guests, save for Lord Kenway who would come to the church to meet with him one on one a few times a month.

Only dire situations warranted such meetings and both men felt that the happenings in their village of Blythe's Hollow were as good of an excuse as any to meet and discuss the issues. The topic of the conversation, to at least start the meeting, was the hanging of the two men from the village that Lord Kenway had caught stealing. The justice that Father Lawrence had served was swift and he was satisfied with the outcome of the day's events.

Lord Kenway was an older man, but to him, his age was nothing but a number. Even at sixty-four he managed to walk around the village, the fields, and farms. He personally inspected the events on his estate and nothing could happen there without his knowledge and say so. He carried on at a good pace; his head held high with pride, though that could be easily called arrogance by a casual observer. That would be the truth; he was an arrogant man, and a greedy one for that matter. He had everything he desired, short of being a king and having his own kingdom, and even that, he still thought to be attainable. It would not be beyond a man like he to try and stage a coup and attempt to oust the current royal family, no matter how absurd the likelihood of succeeding was. He had made his wish to be king known on several occasions, though this had become a joke among the villagers unbeknownst to him.

But on this day, even with his satisfaction duly noted, there was a look of concern on his face. Father Lawrence acknowledged this as Lord Kenway asked him, "You do not think this could spread any further?"

"People are odd creatures, Kenway, there is no answer I could give you that would put your mind at ease," Father Lawrence replied as he twirled his rosary in his wrinkly, bony fingers.

"I know, but I need to be sure that this will not get any more serious than it already is," Kenway said with a frown. "I cannot have simple peasants thinking they have some sort of power or right to do whatever they please. There are rules and everyone has their place. They should know theirs. You know this. I should not be explaining this sort of matter to you."

"I understand your concern, and I can assure you that this interest in witchcraft is just a craze, a phase if you will, that will die down in no time. These are simple peasants. They are trying to explain the existence and the wrath of the pestilence, of this terrible plague, for they do not understand that it is a test sent from God. They are turning to black magick, to the dark arts, and to me, that is a very scary thing."

Lord Kenway nodded and let out a grunt to show his frustration.

"All they have to do is accept that God has a plan for everyone, and for the most part, at least until this plague had come upon us, has been the case of their somewhat decent understanding. But as you see, their way of thinking has changed," Father Lawrence continued.

"I have heard there is a woman, a very old woman, somewhere in the woods, that practices this magick you speak of. It all sounds like a hoax to me," Kenway said. He had ears all over the village and had heard the woman's name on several occasions. Kenway stored this name in the back of his mind, for safe keeping.

Father Lawrence paused for a moment, not surprised at the man's mention of the woman. "Ah yes, I have heard of old Magdalene," he said and smiled. At first, Father Lawrence had thought of her to be a myth, a simple legend or a folklore tale for the villagers to pass their time, but the woman, at least to his knowledge had proven to be real.

"Yes, her," Kenway said.

"I can say she has been a rather nasty thorn in our side. The church would very much like to have her here with us for a conversation."

"As would I," Kenway agreed. "And here I was thinking she was only a legend."

"Oh she is more than merely a legend," Father Lawrence said and shook his head. That same menacing smile was still present on his face and it only hinted at horrible things the church would put Magdalene through if they ever got their hands on her.

"So she really does engage in witchcraft then?" Lord Kenway asked. "I have been told that she is making some sort of potions, mainly with the stolen goods that the villagers have managed to take from my storage. My men have told me that she enchants the peasants, or puts a spell on them, in order for them to do her bidding and steal from me."

"Those are nothing but mere illusions, Kenway, that make the sheep stray from our Lord's path. Like I said, she is a thorn that needs to be dealt with. We cannot have her corrupting the already feeble minds of my flock."

"My men have looked for her," Kenway said. "I have turned the prisoners over and still have no answer as to her whereabouts. It is as if the darkness swallows her whole at any mention of her name. I am having a rather hard time understanding how we cannot find an old woman that lives in the woods and feeds on nothing more than plants. I feel like we have combed the entire isle looking for this wench."

"Perhaps we have to go harder, my friend," Father Lawrence said as ideas went through his head.

"Careful," said Kenway as he shook his gray head in disapproval. "We still need a workforce. We cannot have the entire village killed off. It appears to me the plague is doing that for us."

"I thought of nothing like that, Kenway," Father Lawrence said. "I am merely thinking as a tactician, figuring where we should strike. We must be wise with our resources."

"Agreed," the old man said.

Then came a knock on the door and without even waiting for the reply, Father Williams poked his head through. The two men said nothing; they just stared at the young father in surprise.

"Father Lawrence," said Father Williams, "Can I bother you for a moment of your time?"

Father Lawrence and Lord Kenway exchanged looks and then Lord Kenway patted his belly in preparation to get up.

"Well I better get going, then," said Lord Kenway as he rose from his chair. He nodded at Father Lawrence and added, "As always, I do appreciate your time, Father. Until next time."

"My pleasure," Father Lawrence said, getting up himself. He blessed the old man as he was turning and walking out the door. Then he turned his attention to the young priest who was now cowering in the doorway. He looked like a little mouse about to be snatched by a much larger and more powerful predator; yet there was a glimmer of determination burning in the young man's eyes.

"Yes?" Father Lawrence finally asked, fearing the conversation would never commence if he left it up to Father Williams. "What troubles you, Francis?"

Father Francis Williams was among the youngest of the priests in the church. He was barely thirty years old and was somewhat naive and meek looking, a drawback that the rest of his fellow priests, especially Father Lawrence, used to their own advantage.

Most of his views and opinions, due to his age and inexperience were disregarded and brushed to the side. That is not to say that the man never tried to speak up or fend for himself. No, that was not the case at all; it was just that it was on a very rare occasion that he had someone else on his side. Speaking to Father Lawrence, above all people in the church, was the most nerve wracking. There was something about the man that instilled fear into the young priest, something he couldn't particularly grasp or explain.

Father Lawrence closed the door as he led the young priest out. "Something the matter?" asked Father Lawrence, the tone of his voice flat and devoid of emotion. Perhaps it was this barrier that intimidated the young priest, and would somehow strip him of his defenses.

"I wanted to talk to you... about-" Father Williams attempted to say. His sentence was drawn out, took too long to come out of his mouth, so Father Lawrence cut him short.

"About what, Francis?"

"Well about everything that has been going on in the village. About the hangings...um, the tortures." The young priest spoke nervously, afraid of Father Lawrence's reaction that he could see was already brewing deep inside. The elder very rarely showed his emotions, but when he did, it was just a little to let the other person know that the message was received and to tread carefully.

"What about them?" Father Lawrence asked, surprised, but not entirely. He knew Father Williams was weak, inexperienced, too compassionate in such a troubled time. "Are you against it, Francis? Do matters that we resolve in God's name bother you?"

The young priest noticed the trap so carefully placed by the old man. He pondered his answer before anything came out of his mouth. "Well, it is not that," he began carefully, "it just does not feel right, I mean all the torture, murder. The hangings this morning was something that I believe could have been avoided."

"Have you forgotten 'thou shall not steal' Francis? It appears to me that you have forgotten it indeed. The commandments are not something we can just pick and choose among many which to follow. The rules are simple. They came from our God and they must be followed, no exceptions."

Father Williams began to sweat. "I have not forgotten them," the young priest spoke softly and hung his head low for a moment, almost feeling defeated. "I have not, I just wondered if the punishment, the men being hung was somewhat extreme. Some of the villagers are starving; I see it with my own eyes. I am not defending their actions; I am questioning the punishment."

"It sounds to me that you are questioning God's will," Father Lawrence said and eyed the boy. That was all Father Williams was in his eyes, a mere naïve boy who appeared ready to stray from the righteous path.

"I am not questioning God," Father Williams said a bit more sternly that he even surprised himself. "I am questioning if this is really what He wishes. And I doubt that He does. Does God really want his flock dead? The plague is one thing; I understand it is a test sent to examine our characters, our strength, and devotion. It is my belief that we have taken too much into our hands, took too much liberty to interpret what he really wants, or does not want."

The expression on Father Lawrence's face grew grimmer, his eyes menacing and piercing through young man's very soul. Yet the senior man still kept his composure and the same emotionless tone of voice. "You speak rather ill words that I do not care to hear," he said as they walked down the hall and out of the church.

They stood at the front door and watched as the rain still showered the sad looking village. The day was slowly turning to dusk.

"Who are we to decide what is needed of us or what we should think, Francis?" Father Lawrence asked coldly and not even waiting for the answer to his question, he continued, "This is our calling, these are our lives. We are messengers of God and it is up to us to interpret it to the masses that simply cannot fathom the meaning and the message of His word."

"You mean to tell me that the villagers cannot grasp the meaning of His message?"

"Some can and some cannot."

"So we are putting ourselves onto a higher position in God's eyes than these villagers?" Father Williams said this in a form of a question, almost challenging Father Lawrence.

"I am saying that everyone has their place. God has determined theirs and they have to live out their destined paths, much like we live out ours. We have our place, they have theirs. Transgressors are to be punished, and severely for that matter, Francis. We must set an example of what the consequences are when you go against His word, His will. It is as simple as that."

Father Williams wanted to say the next thing that was on his mind but decided against it. He thought his arguments and opinion to be futile against the elder priest who had been with the church longer than he himself had been alive. He did not like Father Lawrence's answers and he feared that he might say something that would put him even more out of place more than he already was.

39

They stood there in front of a giant wooden and metal gate that led to something that looked more of a torture chamber than a church. Father Williams felt like it had become one.

The rain continued to fall from the dark and fearsome sky and the heat and the sunshine from just a day ago appeared to be a distant memory. Because of the rain, the air had cooled considerably. Father Williams imagined that Heaven continued to cry for the poor souls that have perished over the past few months.

"See, Francis," Father Lawrence said as he looked ahead. "We cannot turn our cheeks the other way as the men and women who have been entrusted to us stray in the direction of the Devil himself. He has called them, and many of them have answered his call of treachery. As you have seen for yourself, this pestilence is not the only thing we are come to battle with. No, for this is only the test of our faith. I'm saddened to see that so many of our own people have turned to the dark arts in their quest for solace. God, Francis, our God, is our only solace, you must remember that."

"Yes, Father," Father Williams said. "But how am I to put my faith in it when all this blood has been spilt? We are here to stop the bloodshed, not further it." Father Williams bowed his head and walked away. As he turned and began to walk, he said, "Excuse me, Father."

Father Lawrence stayed in his place, not uttering a single word nor paying any attention to the young man as he left.

CHAPTER SIX

It was the first time Farah had seen the old woman since she first began hearing the fabled stories. For the most part, they have been true, save for some embellishment tacked on from one story teller to the next.

The woman was old, yes, but how old she could not tell. Was she a hundred? Maybe more? There was no way of knowing and her age, although it was very hard to fall to the task of that observation, was not her priority. Farah had snuck outside the village and went deep into the woods, guided by some personal friends, to an undisclosed location. She was blindfolded for most of her half hour trek through the woods. If someone had asked her to find her way home, she would be unable to do so. She trusted her gut instinct to undertake this task and wondered if that had been a good idea after all.

The witch woman scared her. Farah was uncertain if she was going to kill her in some terrible sacrificial ritual or do something equally sinister.

The steam from a boiling pot in front of her had engulfed Magdalene's old, yet rather smooth face. The woman's long, raven dark hair that was speckled with a few white strands, hung low, almost to the floor, and even though her age was undetermined, the woman appeared to be holding herself rather well. When she opened her mouth to chant some distantly quiet spells and incantations, Farah could see that her teeth were mostly white and healthy, save for one or two. The elder woman appeared to be shrouded in such a mystery that she might not have even been real. And yet here she was, the witch, in the flesh, sitting before her, and casting different sorts of supposed magick.

41

If Magdalene the witch does not get her, Farah thought as she sat there sweating, her only other worry would be the priests and Kenway's men. With everything going on in the village though, she wasn't sure if she really cared. Mixed thoughts coursed through her mind and then she realized it was the woman and the strange environment that was making her uncomfortable. The entire setting raised her awareness level, her anxiety, the fear of the unknown.

Perhaps it was a mistake to have brought Cederic here, Farah thought. She didn't know what to believe. She had heard the stories from others how the witch helped them, how she cured illnesses and how she had brought back the dead. Farah thought it all to be impossible but prayed that it was true. She was desperate to help her father in law and would try anything at this point.

Magdalene looked at Cederic briefly and then blew smoke in his direction as well. She continued to move her lips, emitting strange sounds.

The man was on the verge of death, his life hanging by a thread. He was trying to remain among the living for as long as he could. He was blissfully unaware of his surroundings, Magdalene made sure of that as soon as her visitors stepped into her domain.

Magdalene stirred whatever was in the pot, let the steam rise up above it and then blew it again in the direction of her guests. The young woman coughed, was confused at first, though firmly held her scream. Something inside jerked her, her inner voice screaming for her to flee the old woman's home, and ignore the two men standing there outside the old woman's home that appeared to be some sort of a cottage in a cave.

Suddenly, she relaxed. Her nerves calmed and her heart slowed down as she inhaled the steam from the brewing concoction in the cauldron. Farah became so calm and still, so relaxed that she almost felt as if her soul was levitating outside of her body. For a moment she saw herself sitting there, facing the witch, who now had a book open and was trying to find whatever spell she was going to perform next. When she found what she was looking for, Magdalene glanced at Farah and smirked. The glance was brief, yet powerful, almost binding.

"Your heart is in the right place, dear," the witch said as she waved her hand over the pot. "I will tell you, 'tis very out of place to see such an honest soul in such dark times."

Farah wanted to say something, perhaps explain her situation, the unfair life that she and Edgar were dealt, the brutal violence that surrounded them, the powerful against the weak. The words were lodged in her throat though, perhaps they would release at a later time.

"You must understand something," Magdalene continued, both of her hands now at her side. "Every action we take in life has a consequence. Nothing comes without a price, heed my words. 'Twas always like that, and it shall remain for as long as we are alive and then after we have all turned to ash."

Farah knew the price. She knew it all too well, but as the witch said, her heart was in the right place. She was willing to pay whatever she had, whatever was asked of her.

"But that price doesn't worry you, does it? See, you may not speak out loud, but I can hear you. Perhaps it is better that you not use your words. Most of the time, they are meaningless, just a string of letters that translate into sounds. Actions…now that is what we must focus on. Like you, here, sitting in front of me. Now that is something. Our souls too. Yes, the souls are much more colorful than the words we speak." Magdalene waved her hand again and let more smoke dance its way toward Farah who was now in a catatonic state.

"They say that the disease was sent by whom? God?" the witch scoffed at her own words. "They say 'twas a punishment for your sins. I say nonsense. We lead our lives as we see it fit, for the better or for the worse. Some are destined for good, some for evil. The balance of the light and the dark is within us. That is a battle we must win in our very souls before seeking any kind of divine intervention."

Farah could still see herself, her body sitting there across from the witch. She wondered how much longer this out of body experience would last. She shook her head and realized that the feeling was just the effect of the steam from the cauldron, of the spell, but she didn't care. She felt much more relaxed. She looked at the old woman and could now see her smile for a moment. Magdalene knew that Farah had been anxious; she could smell it on her. Magdalene began to read from the book, then taking her eyes off of it and fixing them on Farah and the man she had brought with her who had been asleep this entire time.

The witch spoke old pagan words, neither English nor Latin but something Farah was sure the church had outlawed many decades ago. The words Magdalene had spoken were unfamiliar to her, odd sounding. Magdalene lifted her arms and directed the steam out of the cauldron and at Farah whose head began to sway back and forth. She was like a puppet and Magdalene was the puppet master. Then everything went black and Magdalene casting her spell was the last thing Farah remembered. How long had she remained in the chasm of darkness, she could not tell. There was no fear in her though, just sheer surprise and marvel.

She came to sometime that night.

****

He did the best he could to follow but ended up losing them somewhere not that far away from Blythe's Hollow. The deeper he went into the forest after the man who led Farah, the more confused and lost he had gotten.

Samuel was good at sneaking around, like a rat he was; this was something extraordinary though. Somewhere, not sure where exactly for everything looked pretty much the same, he had started to get light headed. The forest around him was spinning. It was there that he passed out. When he came to, it was dark and he was alone. Farah and the man were gone. God only knew for how long.

He knew that there was evil in this forest and that losing consciousness was the witch's doing. Oh, he knew it was the wicked Magdalene that had prevented him from going further to find the woman and discover the witch's lair.

It did not matter though; he knew that the woman named Farah was meeting with her, accompanied by some man Samuel had not seen before. Tracking down the location of the witch would have been something that would have gained him much recognition with the other priests. However he did the job, it was his to sneak around the village and expose those who were conspiring with the dark, with the evil forces that led them away from the arms of salvation.

He could feel that evil and darkness in these very woods and being out this late, away from the Church, made him very uneasy. He wondered if something would jump out of the growing shadows and snatch him away into the night never to be seen again.

No, that would never happen he told himself. He was too smart for the fiends of Hell, too sneaky and too valuable to the Church to just perish like that. They needed Samuel. He comforted himself as he walked toward the village. He's the one who exposes those horrible sinners. He's the one that keeps an eye out on the nasty villagers who conspire with the Devil in the night. He's the one who takes care of them when they are brought into the dungeon.

Oh no, the Church would never let anything happen to him.

"I am too valuable, yes I am," he kept repeating to himself as he walked away from the darkness of the woods. "Good ol' Samuel knows where the mischief is. He sniffs out the wrongdoers and he kills them. Oh they all pay in blood for their sins. God loves Samuel for it, he does."

He knew that the spilt blood is for God and knew that the bodies that perish for their sins, by his hand, are the tickets for his own salvation. He would keep doing it as long as he had to, as long as the good Lord demanded that of him. With each sinner gone from this world, he was that much closer to God. With each stab, tear of the flesh, with each ounce of blood dropped on the cold dungeon floors, he was that much closer to the gates of Heaven.

CHAPTER SEVEN

The plague was at work. Edgar looked at the poor woman with disgust, yet a certain degree of pity. Pity, because she was Bradyn's wife and a good woman he had known for a long time. Disgust, because she had come down with buboes all over her body.

He stood there, covering his mouth as the woman took her last breaths. Bradyn sat next to his wife, his face soaked with tears. He held her hand and felt Ella's grip loosening as the woman departed the world of the living.

"I love you, Ella," Bradyn said softly as he kissed the woman's hand and placed it on his forehead. He wanted to continue to cry but there was nothing left. He had dried out like a well on a hot summer day. A single candle burned on the bedside table, casting jagged and distorted shadows on the little room's interior, creating a haunting scene.

Seeing his friend so distraught, Edgar walked over and placed his hand on the man's shoulder. "Her pain is gone, friend," Edgar said quietly. "She is gone and she isn't suffering anymore."

Bradyn disregarded these words and continued to stare at his dead wife. Some of her buboes burst open and as the pus leaked out they also began to bleed, painting the already dirty sheets she had been laying on, red. His stare was blank, devoid of any emotion. It was only his flushed cheeks that gave away the current state of his mind. Yes, he had been crying, but there was much more there than mere sadness. There was anger, confusion, exhaustion, and something else that neither of them could explain.

Edgar squeezed his friend's shoulder and stepped away. There was nothing else he could say to ease Bradyn's pain. Words of comfort were easy enough to come up with, but to actually take them to heart and put them into practice was a different thing entirely. So he decided to remain quiet. He walked back to the other side of the bed and leaned against the wall.

They sat silent for what seemed like an eternity. Bradyn continued to hold his dead wife's hand for a little while longer until he finally set it on the bed and caressed the top of it. He let out a long, painful sigh. It was the sound one of a defeated man. He rubbed his eyes, wiped his face of dried tears, though this didn't do much since his hands had already been covered in dirt from earlier in the day.

Edgar looked at him, waiting for him to say something but Bradyn only stared back at him silently, his eyes growing wider, bigger, his eyebrows raised. Edgar understood the feeling of loss, and he knew, at least to some extent, what Bradyn was going through; but it concerned him seeing his friend like this.

"She's gone," Bradyn finally said, as if this was a newfound fact. He said it coldly. "We should go out and bury her."

"The church will do that," Edgar said, somewhat confused.

Bradyn shook his head as Edgar spoke. He waved his hand in the air as to dismiss the idea. "Absolutely not," he said as he stood up and covered his dead wife with the bed sheet. "What will they do? Come up with some sort of excuse how this was her punishment? They will have her go down as a witch or something."

"Bradyn," Edgar said trying to calm his friend. "I doubt that will be the case."

"How do you know that, Edgar?" Bradyn asked sharply. "I thought you would be the one to understand. Although you never bother to speak your mind loudly, it is safe to say that I have learned your true opinion of the Church and of everything they do, and of everything they have done thus far."

Edgar was silent. There was no denying his dissatisfaction with the events that have transpired in Blythe's Hollow, in its surroundings. Hell, he doubted the situation was much better elsewhere.

"And yet now you have nothing to say, because you know it is the truth," Bradyn said. He walked outside, grabbing the shovel on the way.

Bradyn walked a few steps behind the tiny, crude house until he found a suitable spot to bury his beloved wife in. Edgar followed him, not entirely sure why that particular place was any different from the rest of the unremarkable land that surrounded the shack.

Bradyn began to dig, angrily at first. His movements were violent and melodramatic, but after a few minutes he became weary and slowed down. Edgar watched him with the same level of pity he had observed of Ella earlier. Eventually Edgar took the shovel away from Bradyn and began to dig himself.

Bradyn collapsed on the ground and tried to sob, yet he had nothing left in him, he was beyond exhausted, both physically and emotionally. He was defeated and at that moment wondered if there was anything left to live for. His parents were dead. His only brother was somewhere in London, Bradyn hadn't heard from him in years and often wondered if the man was even still alive. His wife's parents had died in the early days of the plague and now she was dead too. He was all alone.

Edgar looked at Bradyn as he dug, the hole becoming deeper. He knew what Bradyn was thinking, he could see it on his face. He could see it even in the darkness that had engulfed the village. It wasn't hard to know the man's desperation, morbidity, in even such a dark hour of the night.

A man that always exercised caution and did his best not to attract any unnecessary attention had changed in such a short period of time, it was frightening. And he had been right about Edgar not voicing his thoughts out loud. Edgar still had his wife and father to care for, to be cautious for. He cared about them. If any caution and reservation of opinion was exercised, it was for them and them only.

Seeing Farah every day gave him that much more comfort that he would not normally have. Gazing upon her beautiful face after a long and arduous day of labor was what kept him going, what kept him from giving into the desperation and insanity. The knowledge that she was there with him kept his thoughts together. Bradyn, on the other hand, had lost that one bond that kept him whole. He began to fall apart and it was troubling.

Edgar knew that Bradyn would no longer care about his actions and feared that he would merely become one of the dead bodies whose soul would forever be lost in the dark catacombs of the church on the hill above Blythe's Hollow.

Edgar finished digging the grave and then went back inside. He wrapped the deceased woman up in the dirty sheet that Bradyn had covered her with upon her death, then carried her to her final resting place and gently put her in the ground.

Bradyn watched silently and then when Edgar started to bury her, he pushed some of the dirt with his hands in order to help.

"You should come over," Edgar said when they were done covering up the woman's body.

"I do not think I will," Bradyn said and wiped the sweat off his brow. "I think I shall just stay here by myself tonight."

"Are you sure?"

"Yes, I am."

There was a moment of silence. An owl sounded off somewhere not that far away.

"Well, the door is always open," Edgar said and placed his hand on his friend's shoulder.

"I know, thank you," Bradyn said and smiled weakly. "I am just tired. Think I am going to go to sleep as soon as you are gone."

"Are you sure I cannot do anything to make you come with me?"

"I am sure," Bradyn said started walking away. "I am just really exhausted, is all. I will see you tomorrow." He walked back inside and closed the door.

Edgar stared at the makeshift grave, then at the house, and then left without saying another word.

CHAPTER EIGHT

Edgar walked home thinking of Bradyn and his dead wife, and hoped his friend would not engage in any foolish acts that would bring down the wrath of the church on his head. Edgar could understand his friend's suffering, and also understood that it would get significantly worse before getting better.

He opened the door to the house and found Farah sitting in the chair by the candlelight. He was surprised to find her wide awake at this late hour though he was happy that the image of her would be the last one he would see at the end of such a horrid day.

If angels truly existed, they would have her face, he imagined.

"It is late," she said and stood up to greet her husband.

"Yes, I know. I'm sorry."

"I was beginning to worry. I almost came to look for you," Farah said, somewhat relieved.

"Sorry, love."

She hugged him and kissed him on the cheek. Her touch was soft, soothing, relaxing, all of the good things that he could even begin to think of. He closed his eyes briefly and let it linger there.

"Where have you been?" she asked, placing her hand on the small of his back.

Edgar shook his head, hesitating in delivering the answer, something he pondered on the way home. It seemed he brought her nothing but bad news each time he returned home. For once he wished he could say something normal, something that did not involve death, but those were the times that he had forgotten about.

He hesitated a moment longer, then said, "Bradyn's wife, Ella, died today."

Farah watched him in disbelief and placed her hand on her mouth, perhaps in an effort to prevent a shriek or a cry from escaping.

"I was with him. He is rather broken down. I stayed and helped him bury her."

"Oh my," Farah said through her hand.

"He is not doing well," Edgar said and sat down.

"I can only imagine," Farah murmured and lowered herself to Edgar's level. She held onto his arm and kissed his forehead.

"I am worried about him. He looked as if all life was drained out of him. I asked if he wanted to come along, but he just locked himself in his house. I worry he will do something foolish."

"By the sound of it, I am worried as well. And you helped him bury her? That must have been awful!"

"Yes, I did. And yes, I do know it was not my job. If you had seen her, seen *him*, you would have done the same. I could not bring myself to leave her like that, she deserved a proper burial," Edgar said as images of the woman with boils all over her body flashed through his mind. She had lost so much weight; she looked like her skin was hanging off her bones.

"I understand," Farah said and lowered her head. Then she fell silent. Edgar did not come to notice her silence until moments later, and she had already let go of his arm.

She walked slowly to the room where Cederic was sleeping.

"What is wrong?" Edgar finally asked.

She looked at him hesitantly before admitting, "I have done something…"Farah said before she cut herself short. She looked down to the floor as if she was afraid she might get punished if she confessed.

"What?" Edgar asked confused.

"I have done something without your knowledge," she finally continued. "I have done something and I am rather not sure if you will approve."

Edgar slowly stood up, nervous and afraid what else the day might bring him. "What have you done?" His voice was almost a whisper, as if afraid that someone might be eavesdropping.

"I went to see…the woman, the witch, or whatever it is that they call her," she finally said, her head now held high.

Edgar was silent.

Farah opened the door to the room where Cederic had been living out his old age and called to him. The old man appeared, he moved slowly but was at least standing on his own two feet. He used Farah for support for a moment, unsure if he had been dreaming. He looked at Edgar, his son, and smiled.

"Hello, Edgar," the elderly man said as he managed to straighten himself as much as he could. He still held onto Farah, just in case whatever spell he was under decided to leave him.

Edgar stared at his father, then at Farah. Confusion had set in slowly as his legs weakened. He held onto the table, afraid he would faint at the sight of his father walking on his own. At one time, not that long ago, he had wished his father dead, at least to end the poor man's suffering. Now he walked as if something other than his own force was carrying him. Cederic finally sat down.

Edgar reached out and held his father's hand. Cederic cupped his son's hand and held it there. Edgar's hands were cold; perhaps from the sheer shock of seeing him walk, seeing him get up from what was almost a death bed and walk on his own.

"How…how is…" Edgar stammered, tried to find the words. They were there, but could not get out.

Farah smiled. She was happy to see her husband lose his composure in a good way for once. She saw a smile creep out onto his face, his lips slowly curling upward.

"I have done something," Farah said, "something I wondered if you would be upset over."

Edgar looked at his father, then at his wife.

"As I said, I took him to see her and she tended to him and worked her magick," Farah said.

They were all silent. Farah wanted him to say it himself, wanted the words, her name to come out of his own mouth. Perhaps he would be less angry if he had said it instead of her naming the witch.

"The witch? Magdalene?" Edgar finally acknowledged, still holding his father's hand.

Farah nodded. Edgar switched his gaze between the two of them.

"Is it not wonderful?" Farah asked. She still smiled, deep down desperately awaiting her husband's approval.

"It is a miracle, Edgar," Cederic said slowly. "I was beginning to think my time here had expired. But apparently something else...had a different plan for me."

"It is...it's incredible. When did you do this?" Edgar asked.

"Earlier today," Farah said.

Edgar got up and walked to her. He embraced her passionately. He was grateful for what she had done and he wanted her to feel it, to know it. He could tell that there was some concern on her face, even through her smile, that she feared his disapproval. He wanted her to know that it was alright. He wanted her to know that she had done something incredible and that she should embrace her good deed, for it had definitely brightened his depressing day.

"Thank you for this, Farah. You have done well," Edgar said and hugged her for a little while longer.

"She sure has," Cederic said. "You have picked a good woman to bring into our family...as small and dwindling as it is."

Edgar and Farah looked at him, both placing their hands on the old man's shoulders. They felt proud.

"Better times will come," Cederic said. "Sometimes, the only way is to take matters into your own hands. In such times, we become outlaws. Deviants."

Farah walked to the cupboard and took out three bowls to use for dinner.

The last words that Cederic spoke rang in Edgar's head like a church bell.

CHAPTER NINE

Bradyn spent the next morning sitting by and staring at his wife's grave. He spoke to the freshly made mound for some time, ignoring the dim light of the world around him. He spoke to his lost love, the single thread that kept him sane and tied to this world.

He had contemplated suicide for hours after he buried her frail, bloody body. It would have been the easy way out, to end it quick in the middle of a stormy night. It is not like anyone would have noticed. The church would say it was just another soul taken by the Devil himself and the village would accept such a story and everyone would move on.

He cried too; cried for her, he cried because of the emptiness that had crept in so quickly, unannounced. He missed her touch, her smile. Just her being there by his side daily comforted him in this disgusting village. But she wasn't there anymore. The silence, the absence of her soft words and laugh was a painful reminder of the truth.

He now regretted not seeking the help of the witch, like so many others had done. He regretted not taking Ella to see her. He felt weak for not making more effort to heal her battered body, as it fell deeper and deeper into the sickness. The fear of punishment, that perhaps something far more sinister would befall them, if he had taken her to seek the witch's treatment, held him back. There were Kenway's men to worry about, and the priests. The priests that took everyone into their dungeon and cut them to pieces in most brutal ways were the most worrisome. This death was more dignified, he thought.

The fever was the first sign that she brushed aside, thinking she was just coming down with a minor ailment like she had before. Then, unbelievably, the splotches showed up on her beautiful skin and the buboes slowly started to appear on her body, marring her with the face of what they feared most. He thought it would be different, that it could not be Ella that was marked for death. His denial that his beloved was being ravaged by the pestilence would be their downfall.

He now knew he was wrong.

She is in a better place now…he told himself over and over again. But was she really? Was she really in a better place or was it just a simple delusion to make himself feel better? He knew one thing and that was that her place was with him. That was the better place of the two.

The day he met Ella was when everything changed for him. Ella was seventeen, and already a beautiful woman. He had been beaten badly in a quarrel with some local bandits, and left out in the woods to bleed out. One of his eyes was so swollen he could barely see through the thickness of it. What the fight was about, he could not remember. It did not even matter now. It did not even matter anymore at the very moment he laid his eyes on her. She had been walking with her friend and by some crazy chance just happened to stumble upon his broken, bloody body. He passed out shortly after she started to wipe his face with the hem of her dress.

It was their first day together. He was a complete stranger to her at the time, but that did not stop her from coming to his aid in his dire time of need. He had asked her on several occasions how she could help out a stranger like that and she would always say that, "He was a handsome stranger." She would smile when she would say this and that is when he would think about all the blood, cuts and bruises on his face.

Ella would say she was not looking at his face. They would both laugh and hug each other through the night. They never had much in terms of material possessions but that was alright by Ella. She knew it would be next to impossible for people like them to be rich and she never dreamed of such a life. To her, it was to love or be wealthy. You are born into one or the other, she would often say, and she was happy that with them, it was love.

They warmed each other on the cold nights, she cooked, and he fixed things around their humble house, all while playing a slave along with other villagers of Blythe's Hollow. The life outside of their home was bleak and morbid. He went to the fields, the woods, and the mill with other villagers, toiling at back breaking work from sunrise to sunset.

He would return home, cut and bruised from the intense labor and weather conditions. He would ache all over, not being able to move the rest of the night, but at least she was there to comfort him in body, mind, and spirit. Ella made sure she was that small solace and support he needed at the end of the day. She made sure she was there for him and though she could not provide much, she gave her love, her body, and her soul. To Bradyn, that was all that mattered. The life inside the house was wonderful, easy, for the walls of the home were barriers that guarded against the ugliness of the outer world. Inside, they could have anything, be anyone.

And now, Ella was no longer among the living. That void sent tremendous pain through his heart. He then started to cry. He wondered why he did not mention anything to Edgar and Farah when Ella came down with the sickness. Perhaps it was pride. Or then again it could have been fear that it would come out through gossip in the village and she would be taken away from him. It did not matter, now that she was gone.

He sighed, tossed a look at the dirty, muddy shovel and rubbed the area under his arm that had been itching all morning. It hurt once he touched it. He peeked into his shirt and saw that he developed the same type of sore that Ella had. He felt it again, probing it further and this time a bloody and pus-like residue got on his fingers as the boil burst.

Given the different circumstances, he might have been scared, but at this moment, he merely looked at the sore some more, wiped his fingers off on his shirt and resumed his vigil at the grave. *So*, he thought, *his time had come too.* That was fine with him.

Then suddenly Bradyn heard a noise coming from behind him. In defense, he went for the shovel, grabbing it.

"No need for that, my friend," the voice came from behind. When Bradyn saw who the voice came from, he was ready to strike. He planted his feet firmly and almost pounced at the man standing there in front of him.

"What are you doing here?" Bradyn asked, clenching his fists around the shovel.

"There is no need for that. I have come in peace, Bradyn," Father Williams said and raised his arms, ready to surrender. "I have come alone. No one is here except me. I doubt anyone even knows I am here."

Bradyn was somewhat confused, even caught off guard. These men have rarely ever come this deep into the village, and when they did, they usually had three or four of Kenway's guards with them. This young priest was here by himself, or so he said. Regardless, Bradyn continued to hold the shovel like a sword, ready to strike.

There was a moment of silence. Father Williams slowly lowered his arms. He was young, pale…even paler in the direct sunlight. He looked different than the others were Bradyn thought. He looked less menacing than his counterparts.

"Really, you can relax. I am not here to fight. And if I was, I am sure you could kill me without much effort."

Bradyn relaxed a little, but continued to eye the man up and down. The bottom of his robe was dirty, caked in mud.

"I have been walking around the village today. I have been meeting the people, seeing how everything is down here," Father Williams said, and then paused. "How rude of me, I have forgotten to introduce myself. My name is Francis."

"Bradyn," Bradyn finally said. "I am Bradyn. What brings you to this hellish place, Father? We do not see priests venturing down here unless it is with the Lord's guards and swords all around you. I must say, we are certainly not use to seeing the likes of you out and about alone."

Francis sighed. "It is a bad stigma that follows us, it is true. We are meant to spread the loving word of the Lord, not drive our people away from him."

"He has left us long ago, Father. That is, if he had ever been here," Bradyn scoffed and replaced the shovel into the dirt. "I am sure you have seen the misery on your travels today. You have seen it for one day. This is what we wake up to *every* day."

Francis stood there, silent.

"Forgive me for being direct, but this is one flock that is going down a different path, Father. If I were you, I would turn and go back up that hill and into your chambers."

Francis looked at the fresh grave that Bradyn was standing next to. His eyes trailed there and Bradyn noticed it.

"My wife," Bradyn said. "I assume you will report this back to whoever arranges the tortures and murders. You can go right ahead and do so. I have nothing to fear."

"You misunderstand why I am here," Francis finally said. "I remind you once more Bradyn that I have come in peace. I am here to do what little I can to restore your faith into an institution that has failed you thus far. I am not here as a spy, nor will I report any wrong doings that the Church might hunt you and punish you for."

Now it was Bradyn's turn to be silent.

"At least let me help you give your wife a proper burial. She deserves at least that much, would you not agree?"

Bradyn shook his head. "This is as proper as it will get, Father. Will you leave me to my misery? I doubt I have much time left as it is." He lifted his shirt and showed the young priest his sore. Bradyn had become sweaty, looking like he was beginning to come down with the fever.

Francis, startled by what he saw, took a step back, covering his mouth in horror. His expression was the one Bradyn expected. Bradyn almost laughed at the man and his somewhat comical reaction. Not that the revelation itself was comical, but just the mere reaction from the young man.

"Is this God's judgment, Father? Is it?" Bradyn asked. "Was I not a decent human being? Was my wife an evil wretch? Is our life of survival in such misery a warrant for a death sentence?"

"Let me help you, Bradyn!" Francis had now regained his composure and stepped toward Bradyn, reaching out with one hand while holding onto the cross hanging from his neck with the other.

Bradyn laughed. "Help? Help me with this? Oh you naïve man! Leave now and save yourself while you can. This is a disease, it was not sent by God. It is just a disease. That is all it is. I see that now. It is not some punishment from God for whatever it is that we did wrong or for our supposed sins. It is a pestilence that spreads from one man and woman to another without any discrimination. Are you so blind that you do not see this? Is it your ignorance or stupidity, or is it perhaps both?"

"Bradyn, please," Francis implored but Bradyn just waved him off.

"Leave, Father. God is not here with us. Live your life while you can." Bradyn sat down where he was sitting earlier and stared at the grave again.

Francis, hesitant at first, walked to the broken man and placed a hand on his shoulder. "We all go through our own personal Hell," Francis said. "We have full control to let the others in and allow them to help us, Bradyn. You may have lost sight of God, but He has not lost sight of you."

"Then why is He letting all this happen?" Bradyn asked. "The God you believe in does not exist. It is the people that are evil, Father. Not God, not the Devil-"

Before he could finish his sentence, four armed guards, Kenway's men, rode in on horses, brandishing their swords. Before either man realized what was going on, the soldiers had surrounded them, mainly focusing on Bradyn.

Bradyn jumped up from his spot and snatched the shovel. He passed an angry look at Francis.

"Bradyn, please believe me...I did not-"

"Save it. You are all the same," Bradyn said. He was already in his fighting stance, eyeing the man, anticipating an attack to come from any given direction. The odds of his survival were minimal; the guards were clad in their armor and they had their swords. He turned this way and that, trying to keep up with them. He swung the shovel in an attempt to keep them away.

Father Williams tried to talk to the soldiers but the commotion was too great for anyone to pay attention. They were all fixed on the man defending himself with a garden tool.

"Come on!" Bradyn snarled. "Come and taste the death. I have got plenty for all you sorry bastards!" He swung the shovel and almost hit the guard closest to him.

"Men, please calm down! What are you doing here?" Father Williams called out to them.

"We are here to bring him in, Father Williams. He along with few others."

"On whose authority?" Father Williams demanded.

"On mine," came the voice from behind. "He is to be brought in for questioning, Father Williams," Father Lawrence replied as he stepped next to the young man.

"You have been followed, Francis," he said. "I have seen what you have tried to do and yet you still fail to comprehend the hopelessness of this situation. You fail to realize that we are at war and you are walking a fine line between the dark and light sides."

"What are you doing? This man has done nothing wrong," Father Williams said standing his ground. "Please, call them off."

"On the contrary, Father Williams, this man has done enough to warrant his capture. You know that we have eyes everywhere and no deed done in this village escapes the ever reaching hand of justice."

"This is preposterous!" Father Williams exclaimed.

"Careful, Francis," Father Lawrence warned the young man.

Behind the priests, Bradyn continued to swing his shovel and actually managed to hit one of the guards, knocking him off his horse. Another guard came to his fallen comrade's aide and Bradyn swung at him too, missing but still keeping the man at bay. The fallen man then got back up and lunged with his sword barely missing him. Bradyn, turning into a fighter he did not believe he could ever be, countered and hit the man on the side of his head. He could hear the skull cracking. Blood burst forth from the split in the skin and poured down the man's face as he collapsed, probably dead by the looks of him.

"Restrain him!" Father Lawrence yelled from behind.

"Please stop!" Father Williams countered.

"You will have to kill me to take me, you shite." Bradyn spit. Catching him off guard, one of the guards managed to come from behind; he hit Bradyn with the handle of his sword, knocking him unconscious. Bradyn sprawled out next to his wife's grave as Kenway's guards stared at him. One of them was on the ground, and the other three panted, trying to catch their breath.

"This is your warning, Francis," Father Lawrence said sternly. "You are walking through a battlefield and ready to show everyone quarter. Your guard is down and your faith is too weak. Heed my words, Francis. You will not meet a desirable end to your life if you continue on the path you have chosen."

"And what path is that?" Francis asked.

Father Lawrence regarded him a moment longer then raised his index finger and pointed it at the young man. "Heed my words."

CHAPTER TEN

Edgar and Farah woke up to yelling and commotion not too far from their home. The sun had already cast its early rays onto the village and had started to come through the cracks in the wooden shutter covering the window opening of their house and shone directly into Edgar's face, blinding him for a moment. He shielded his eyes as he struggled to get off the bed, still fresh out of his dream, his legs weak and wobbly.

Farah had already gotten up and was at the door of their room. She cracked it open and was peeking into the living area.

"What is going on?" Edgar asked, putting on his shirt and pants.

"I do not know! Sounds like the whole village is about to fight!"

"Let me go see what the fuss is about," Edgar instructed as he gently moved her aside so that he could get out of the room. "Do not come out until I tell you. Understand?"

She nodded without saying a word.

Cederic woke up too and was standing at door of his tiny room. He was propping himself against the side of it.

"Be careful, my son," he called out after Edgar.

"Go lay back down, we do not want anyone to see you," Edgar said and motioned to him to go back inside his room. Edgar had no idea what was happening outside and he did not want to take any risks. Everyone in the village knew that Cederic was almost crippled and practically on his death bed. Edgar knew that if anyone saw Cederic now and his miraculous recovery, especially Kenway's men, there would be trouble to be had.

He gave a look to his wife, and then his father in an attempt to reassure them and let them know everything would be fine. His heart pounded and his hand on the door latch shook, Edgar paused and took a deep breath before opening the door.

He finally pulled it open to see the battle that was unfolding outside. The villagers of Blythe's Hollow were up in arms; some men carried their pitchforks, others had shovels and clubs, while one or two even carried old swords they might have stolen and stashed away a while ago. Kenway's men led the way on horse. There were eight of them on horseback, their swords pulled out, ready to cut down anyone who stood in their way. Behind the riding guards, two more followed on foot, carrying crossbows. Following them, bringing up the rear, was Kenway himself accompanied by some members of the clergy, most notably Father Lawrence and Father Johns.

Edgar looked again at his wife and father. "Do not come out!" he said, and then walked outside and shut the door behind him.

He saw a villager, swinging his club around, come out into the street and attack one of the horsemen but he was easily struck down by the swing of a sword. The man fell, his shoulder splayed open. He struggled to stand back up yet it was too late. He was trampled by the horses as he reached for his lost weapon. At the last moment, before he could even look away, Edgar saw the man's head get crushed under the hooves of the giant beast. Bits and pieces of his skull and brain scattered as villagers protested in horror. The guards, Lord Kenway, and the priests continued onward.

"What the hell is going on?" Edgar asked the first villager he could stop from passing him by.

"An uprising," he said. "That is what! We will not stand for this anymore." The man broke free from Edgar's hold and joined in the crowd moving to stand against the guards.

"They have been taking people," another villager said. He stood close to Edgar and observed the conflict. "Taking them prisoners. They have had spies among us, my friend, exposing our struggle that apparently goes against the church."

"What?" Edgar said, not sure if he was hearing the man correctly or if it was simply that he could not believe what he was hearing.

"They are taking people suspected of black magick, conspiring with the Devil, the evil spirits or what not. It has all gone to shite," the man

63

said. "See those standing there, not really moving or anything? Right behind Kenway, in front of that house?"

"Yes," Edgar said. "What about them?"

"Those are the ones. The ones that report everything to Kenway and the Church. How do you think they have sniffed everything out?"

Two peasant men tried to attack from the side but the guards fired their crossbows and pierced them in the head. The arrows flew through their eye sockets, coming out through the other side of their skulls.

"They cannot do this..." Edgar said, but not really sure why or if it made any sense. Of course they can. They could do whatever they wanted.

"And who is there to stop them?" the man asked and laughed. It was a crazy laugh.

It was now that Edgar noticed that there were prisoners, villagers in shackles being dragged behind the armed column. There were three of them. He had seen them around but did not know their names. It did not matter now. They would be dead soon.

The guards moved in Edgar's direction, slowly but surely as the scattered attacks on them have subsided.

"Edgar Smith!" Lord Kenway yelled to be heard over the crowd of villagers. "Edgar Smith!" he yelled again and stepped forward with Fathers Lawrence and Johns.

Edgar's heart stopped for a moment and dropped into his stomach. He swallowed hard, with an effort, as if something was lodged in his throat.

"Step out front, Edgar," Father Lawrence said. "Your wife, Farah, has been charged with conspiring and dabbling in witchcraft. Her waywardness has gone against everything that our Church stands for and for that she must be punished." Father Lawrence spoke in his calm, yet authoritative voice.

Edgar began to slowly move backwards, in a feeble attempt to not attract any attention to himself. To his horror, several villagers turned their heads in his direction. This was noticed by the guards and most notably Father Lawrence, who now whispered something to Lord Kenway. The fat man nodded in approval.

They saw him move and now they were coming to get Farah. His legs felt weak; he wanted to move faster, turn around and run inside, get his wife and run away. He screamed at himself inside his head to get moving.

Finally he turned, not caring anymore who saw him. They would come to the house eventually; it was just a matter of time. He ran as swiftly as he could, winding his way through the village until he reached his home. Breathlessly Edgar ran inside, shut the door and went to Farah who had been waiting for him patiently. Cederic was once again in his bed.

"What is going on?" Farah asked. Concern was there; clearly outlined on her face, though even in the gravest circumstances it remained naturally beautiful.

"That was faster than I would have expected," Edgar said as he pushed her to their room. "They have found out about what you did!" He then went to his father's room and started to get him out of the bed.

"Leave me," Cederic said.

"They are coming to get you, Farah," Edgar continued. "We need to get you and dad out of here."

"Oh dear," Farah said as she grabbed some rags off the bed. Edgar propped his father up and was helping him walk. The voices on the outside grew louder by the second.

"We need to get out. We will use the back window," Edgar said.

"And go where?" Farah asked puzzled. She was frustrated and concerned, but the fear that Edgar expected to see was still not there. She had to have expected such an outcome.

"Anywhere but here," Edgar answered and shut the door to their room. A small armoire that they used to keep their meager possessions was in the corner of the room. Edgar left Cederic for a moment to take it and move it against the door.

"Leave me, Edgar," Cederic instructed. "What use is there for you to risk your lives for me? My time has come, my son."

"I am not leaving you!" Edgar said sternly, put his father's arm over his shoulder, and moved him to the window.

Farah went out first, then Cederic. The old man fell down and groaned in pain. By the time Edgar was climbing up through the window, the front door of the house had been broken down and the guards were now inside. He heard the commands given by Kenway and the priests to hurry and find the woman and the elder man.

When Edgar made it out, Farah and Cederic were already some distance ahead. They stopped to look back at Edgar who was now running after them. He waved them on but the two refused to move until he fully caught up to them.

"Go!" Edgar almost yelled. "They are already in the house." He took over the task of helping Cederic move and then they continued on together as fast they could. The older man groaned and panted.

"Come on!" Edgar urged them. "We have got to make it to the woods."

An arrow hissed through the air. The next thing Edgar heard was his father's low, guttural grunt. The force of the bolt had pushed Cederic forward causing Edgar to lose his grip on him. Cederic collapsed, crying out in pain. The projectile had hit him right in the middle of his back. A quick glance and Edgar could see that it was lodged in there rather deep.

Farah screamed as she watched Cederic crumple to the ground, blood already trickling down his back. The man whimpered in pain, his face contorted with anguish. He began to lose his breath as he tried to speak.

"No, do not say anything," Edgar advised as he tried to pull the arrow from his back but Cederic winced at the slightest touch.

"I...I cannot...feel my legs..." he panted, blood now bubbling forth and coming out of his mouth too. He coughed and spewed the vital fluid onto the grass in front of his face, turning it dark red like the floor of a butcher's shed.

"It is pretty deep in there!" Edgar said, his emotions all thrown in a hot cauldron, mixing with fear, anger, anxiety, desperation. "Damn it! Damn it!"

"Edgar, they are coming. Look!" Farah said, her voice filled with terror. "We have to go now. Let us pick him up!"

"No," Cederic mumbled around his fluid filled mouth. "It is too late for me. Go..." he said again, spitting more blood. "Too late for...the old man...to go...on further. This...is where I will...rest."

"No, I can carry you!" Edgar protested and tried to lift his beloved father, but the frail, wounded man resisted and pushed his son away, hacking up more blood in the process. The ground below him was soaked in a scarlet pool from the sanguine fluid now gushing from his mouth and back.

Farah crouched down and kissed the elder man's head. "We love you," she said, tears running down her face. "We love you, Cederic. Go in peace." She looked at Edgar and placed her hand on his arm. "Love, we have to go."

"Leave," Cederic instructed. "You must…save yourself. What good…will an old…man do for…anyone?"

Edgar hesitated, anger seething through his teeth. His face transformed right there on the spot, into something evil, sinister, and full of hatred. Farah had never seen him like this before and for a moment, he scared her. Kenway's men were approaching fast. One of them fired another arrow which flew right past Edgar's head and twanged into a nearby tree.

He turned his father and kissed him on the forehead. "You will be forever with me," Edgar said, a single tear trailing down his left cheek. Farah tugged on his arm. Edgar got back up to his feet and started running along with his wife, every now and then looking back at his dying father. When they made it to the tree line of the forest, the couple stopped and watched as Kenway's men carried Cederic away.

Edgar became silent and stoic. The anger that was previously on his face disappeared, melting away in to a rigid and determined look. His now calm and resolute demeanor was even more sinister than the fiery attitude of before. Farah had always known him to be a composed and calculated man, one to only say what needed to be said and nothing more. Though he had had every right to be angry and upset, much like she was, there was something very different about him now.

Still hidden, carefully they watched the guards carry Cederic and when one of them pointed at the fleeing couple, three of them began to move in their direction.

Without further hesitation, Edgar and Farah turned and began to move deeper into the woods.

CHAPTER ELEVEN

Bradyn woke up some time later to find himself stripped down to his pants. It did not take him long to figure out that he was in one of the torture chambers beneath the church and that he was hanging from the ceiling. His hands were tied by chains and he hung just low enough to touch the cold floor with the tip of his toes.

So this was how everything was going to end? He asked himself in his head, with a laugh almost escaping him.

His skull ached a little from his earlier encounter with the guards. Some blood had been trickling down the side of his scalp but had dried since. He could feel it there, all tight and crusty. He turned his head side to side in an effort to relax his neck muscles and in the process of doing so, witnessed all the bloody contraptions that were placed around the room.

There was a gory iron maiden in the corner to his right. Fresh blood was dripping from the sharp metal spikes. Torn meat and flesh hung there too. Chunks of the previous victim ripped off the torso as the corpse was pulled out of the nightmarish torture device.

Next to the iron maiden was a tiny cell, perhaps big enough to fit a child. Inside was a body, not fully decomposed yet, but most certainly dead. He could see the deep cuts and gashes all over the poor bastard. The man, or what was left of him in there, had to have gone through Hell and back at the hands of murderous staff.

He did not look around any further. They were going to do whatever it was they were going to do to him, and the sooner he accepted it, the faster everything was going to pass. It was not like he had any chance at escaping this morbid place. The priests were going to come in, let him know of all the sins he had committed and how all of that went against their teachings. He felt as though that would be more of a torture than actually being cut and beaten.

And then, as if on cue, the door to the torture chamber opened and Father Johns walked in, followed by Father Lawrence and another shorter, sickly looking man. He knew this monk was the one actually getting his hands dirty. The last to walk in was a fat man with a hood over his face and robes that were soaked in the blood and bits and pieces from his earlier victims.

"Hello, Bradyn," Father Lawrence said. Father Johns shook his head in disapproval of Bradyn's actions, whatever those were. Bradyn did not greet them back, choosing to remain silent in defiance.

"I am sure you know why you are here, Bradyn," Father Johns said. Father Lawrence and the pale monk were in the back, the priest whispering something to the smaller man. The little monk nodded, and then walked over to the fat, robed man.

"You choose not to answer this?" Father Johns asked. "This is a serious matter, Bradyn, and your salvation is my priority." He paused for a moment, eyed him up and down and then said, "I am here to help you."

"Oh please," Bradyn said sarcastically and rolled his eyes. He scoffed and looked the other way.

"Do you mock me?" Father Johns asked. "Do you mock our faith? Our Church?"

"You have no authority over me," Bradyn said as calmly as he could. "You have no authority over anyone. You think yourself so high and mighty, standing there, judging me, when one day, you all shall be judged for the atrocities you have committed."

"Blasphemy06" Father Lawrence exclaimed as he approached and stood beside Father Johns

"How dare you?" Father Johns raised his voice. "You mock us even mere moments before your death? Have you nothing to say to save yourself?"

"Untie me so I can choke the life out of you."

Father Johns stepped back, clearly appalled by Bradyn's remark, while Father Lawrence simply stood there as he was, not particularly moved by the harsh statement.

"We now confirm our fears that your soul shall burn in Hell for all eternity, Bradyn," Father Lawrence said. "God is our witness that we have tried to help you, to save you from the fiery pits and in this last moment, we have failed you."

"I welcome the fiery pits over this godforsaken place," Bradyn said and laughed. He then clenched his teeth in anger.

"You shall die now, sinner," Father Johns said and motioned to the large man who walked over and began to untie Bradyn. The man wrapped one of his arms around Bradyn's waist and untied him with the other. Bradyn took this opportunity to deliver a powerful blow to the back of the man's head, staggering him. He let go of Bradyn who fell but quickly got back to his feet.

"Brother Samuel!" Father Lawrence yelled at the small monk. The little man tried to step up to Bradyn but was easily pushed away. Bradyn managed to get a hold of Father Johns. Father Lawrence stepped aside just in time, leaving Father Johns by himself. Bradyn quickly wrapped his hands around Father Johns throat and squeezed tight, so tight that his thumbs began to dig into the flesh and blood started to seep out of the torn skin as the man tried to scream. Then, the pitiful attempts at screaming, turned to painful gurgling as Bradyn pushed harder and further into the man's throat, gouging into the muscles and vital arteries. By the time the lumbering executioner got back to his feet, Bradyn's thumbs were deep in Father Johns throat, silencing his cries for help. The fat man kicked Bradyn in the lower back, causing his knees to buckle and give out. He sprawled out on the floor and let go of the dying man. Father Johns clutched at his throat, blood cascading out of it like a fountain. Father Lawrence came to his aid but it was too late. Father Johns collapsed into the bath of his own blood. Father Lawrence looked at his fellow priest, then closed his eyes and crossed himself.

The executioner held Bradyn against the wall with one hand around his throat and began hitting him in the face with the other. After three powerful blows, the man released him

and watched him wobble there for a moment. Samuel came rushing forward and grabbed Bradyn by his arms to lead him to the stretching table. Without much effort, the executioner lifted Bradyn up and placed him on the stretcher, spreading him out. Placing his arms in their full length above his head like he was about to reach for something. Samuel began to strap Bradyn's wrists and ankles into leather belts, almost giggling in the process.

"You will be punished, sinner!" Samuel exclaimed.

Bradyn was conscious enough to turn and spit on the man, right in his face, coating it with saliva and blood. Samuel took a step back, stunned and angry. He wiped the filth off with his sleeve, approached Bradyn again and stared him right in eyes, their noses almost touching.

"I promise you," he giggled again, "that you will be in so much pain…" Samuel clenched his fist, not knowing what else to say.

The executioner started to turn the wheel that wound up and stretched the ropes attached to Bradyn's limbs. Little by little, Bradyn's body extended with each limb being pulled in opposite directions. He began to cry out in pain.

Samuel laughed.

****

Father Francis Williams sat in his room and listened to the screams coming from the torture chamber. He sat there, hands on his knees, staring at the wall. He winced each time Bradyn screamed, but as the screams became longer and more painful, Francis stopped his wincing and merely continued to gaze blankly at the wall.

There was a simple wooden cross hanging in front of him. His rosary was in his one hand draping over his knee. He prayed and begged God to come to his aid, to answer his questions and alleviate his confusion. He prayed for Bradyn's end to come quick, for his death to be without pain, but he knew that it was not going to happen. Bradyn's suffering was abhorrent and cruel, he was being stretched, slowly ripped apart and was only mere moments away from a gruesome death. There was nothing Francis could do to stop it.

He stared at the cross, scrutinizing it intensely, as if he was having some sort of mental battle with it. And then, something inside of him snapped, and he let the rosary fall to the floor.

He stood up from his bed, walked over to the cross, took it off the wall and threw it on the floor. He shuddered and wondered if some divine power would come down to punish him, if God himself would send the angels down to rip his soul apart. Yet nothing happened. He stood there and surveyed the now broken little wooden cross on the floor.

Bradyn continued to scream.

Francis then pulled the hood over his head and walked out of the room.

****

Bradyn could both feel and hear his muscles tear apart, his bones slowly fissure and break. It was a terrible pain, one he could only imagine in his worst nightmares.

He screamed at the top of his lungs, as loud as his vocal cords would allow him. He cursed his tormentors. One of his legs dislodged itself from the hip, then the other. The executioner kept twisting the wheel, winding the ropes, pulling them tighter, stretching Bradyn's body further and further apart, rupturing bone, muscle, sinew, and skin. Then with one last pull, Bradyn's legs and arms were torn off from his torso. Blood squirted in every single direction, splattered the walls, Samuel, and the executioner. Bits and pieces of flesh and bone flew wildly around as the body was ripped apart.

His agonizing screams stopped in an instant.

CHAPTER TWELVE

Edgar and Farah weaved their way between the trees as they ventured further into the woods. He held her hand firmly in his and every time he felt her trailing behind, he would pull her closer. Now and then they would stop for a moment, catch their breath and then continue onward.

Farah eventually stopped, bent over and panted heavily. Not realizing her current state, Edgar tried pulling her forward, despite her resistance. They had been on the run for hours and although he thought that they lost Kenway's guards, there was still that smidgen of doubt at the back of his head and he was eager to continue.

"I cannot," she gasped while trying to catch her breath. She was caked in sweat and dirt and so was he. "I have to take a break and sit down for a little bit."

"Alright," Edgar said hesitantly. "Let us rest." It was now dark and the only source of illumination was the moonlight coming through the trees.

"I am so thirsty," Farah said as she propped herself up against the tree. Her legs were weak from the previous hours of exertion; she slid down the trunk and collapsed.

"We shall take a break and continue shortly then," Edgar replied then paused and looked in the direction they were headed in. "I think the creek is that way. I believe I can hear it, should not be too far now."

He sat down next to her and placed his arm around her shoulders. They sat in silence for a while, listening to the sounds of the forest. An owl sounded off somewhere in the distance and the crickets sang their songs all through the night.

"I am sorry," Farah finally whispered, breaking the peaceful silence.

"For what?" Edgar asked.

"For seeking the help of the witch. Magdalene."

Edgar shook his head and then realized he was only doing that to himself and that she could not see it. "You have nothing to be sorry about, love," he finally said as he kissed the top of her head. Even though they were on the run for a while now, her hair still smelled good. It put him at ease.

"None of this would have happened," she said.

"It would have, eventually. You never know with them. There is always something to bring their wrath upon us. I love you for doing what you did. For at least a very short time, my father regained some of his dignity." Edgar smiled and then continued, "I loved seeing him walk on his own. I think I even saw some happiness in his eyes when he took the steps into the room. Even when he ran away from the guards on his own…it had done a great deal for him."

Edgar's voice was mellow, soothing once again. Farah enjoyed it and the fact that he was not angry with her, just made everything a little better.

"I love you," she said softly.

Edgar was silent for a moment, taking it in. He had forgotten how much those three little words meant to him, how much she meant to him. He smiled at her and she saw his face in the moonlight. She smiled back.

"I love you too," Edgar said and leaned in for a kiss. Their lips locked in and he pulled her in tight. They stayed like that for a minute.

To them, it was an eternity.

She then rested her head on his chest. Farah started to hum a song that her mother always sang to her when she was just a child. The reverie made her feel nostalgic. She longed for a family with Edgar, to hold a child of her own. But the times were not right. How could she bring a child into such a cruel world? The God that was supposed to protect them from evil was not there, and in his place were men preaching what they called his word, his will. How could that be? She continued to think through her song.

No, God really wasn't there with them.

"Are we going to be alright, Edgar?" she asked, stopping her song.

"We will, love," Edgar said, his head against the tree with his eyes closed.

"How can you be so sure?"

He paused, taking a moment to search for the right words. Then, when he found them, he said, "Because we will. Things are in our own hands. We will make it all work."

"I trust you," she said.

"I will never leave you," Edgar said. "That's a promise, and you know me, I do not make promises I cannot keep."

She smiled again. He could feel her face tightening on his chest. "I know."

"We shall run away somewhere, far away from here and build ourselves a little cabin. You can have a beautiful garden in the back for your flowers. We will not tell anyone where we live and we shall keep everything a secret, so no one can ever bother us."

"And have children, right? We can finally have children? I would like a daughter."

"Of course we can." Edgar now smiled too. He always wanted children, but like they agreed before, it just was not the time.

"I would name her...Lorelle," Farah said happily.

"That is a good name for a girl," Edgar said. "What about a boy?"

"We can have a boy too."

"What would we name him?" Edgar asked.

"How does Raymond sound to you?" She asked.

"A very strong name," Edgar said. "I like it."

"Well that settles it then," Farah said. "We can have Lorelle and Raymond."

"That sounds wonderful. Those are perfect names."

"And they will be great children," Farah said. "They will take on our best qualities and grow up to be great people."

Edgar did not know what to say to that. The story that they were telling themselves was wonderful, uplifting, but it was just a story. Farah was happy, it is what mattered. Perhaps it would get her through the next part of their escape, keep her spirits lifted. The story was so good that Edgar could almost picture everything as if it were all right in front of him. A small house, children's laughter, a content wife...

It was idyllic. They talked into the night until they both fell asleep.

Edgar woke up with the first rays of light. He slowly came to and realized that they had been asleep a lot longer than he had wanted. Without further hesitation, he nudged Farah to wake up. "Love, we have to go. Come on, wake up," he said and kept nudging her. Kenway's guards could have been on top of them in the middle of the night and they would not have even known. They could have had their throats cut and that would have been the end of them.

"Edgar," she said groggily.

"We must go, we have to keep moving, love. Let us go."

"Alright," Farah said getting up. "How long were we asleep?"

"Too long. I do not want to wait any longer to find out if they continued searching for us or not." Edgar was up and pushing her forward.

They walked for barely a minute when an arrow hissed through the air, and Edgar did not hear it until it the pain seared through his arm. He felt the arrow lodge itself right into his shoulder. He yelled in agony and pushed Farah ahead.

"Edgar!" she yelled and went back to him.

"*Go!*" he screamed at her then looked in the direction the shot had come from. Two of the guards were there. They must have been walking the entire night following their trail.

The guards approached them. One of them carried the crossbow and had it pointed at the couple. The other guard had his sword out.

"It will be alright," Edgar told his wife.

"Edgar," she said. "I am afraid." She held him tightly. He felt the arrow in his shoulder and pulled it out. This time he grunted painfully, keeping his voice inside. Blood rushed out and Farah fumbled her hands over the wound, blood squirting on her dirty dress.

"You have to come with us," the guard with the sword said. "We have been instructed to bring you dead or alive and it makes no difference to us."

"I would prefer dead," the one with the crossbow said.

"We could definitely have some fun with the woman first. You know, before we kill them." The one with the sword got closer to them and pointed it at Edgar. "We make him watch first, then kill them both."

"I get the first turn with her," the crossbow man said.

"What gives you the authority to decide?" The sword man turned and looked at his friend.

Edgar used their argument to hit the man closer to him in the back of his leg, buckling his knee at the impact. The guard's leg gave out, opening the way and giving Edgar enough time to kick him in the face. The man fell down, holding his face in pain.

The one with the crossbow fired another arrow but missed Edgar. Farah screamed but Edgar paid no mind to her in the heat of the moment. He ran toward the crossbow man and tackled him to the ground. Edgar got on top of him in one fluid motion and began hitting him in the face with both hands as more blood gushed from his wound. When the man dropped his weapon and Edgar realized he posed no further threat, he got up and turned to Farah.

She sat where he had left her, holding the arrow jutting out of her stomach. Her dress was soaked in blood. She panted, trying to speak but each time she did, she winced and swallowed her words.

"Farah!" Edgar ran to her and slowly laid her down on the ground. "Do not talk love, save your breath. It will be alright, I promise. It will be alright."

"Edgar…" she said weakly.

"Shhhh," Edgar put his finger on her lips. "Do not talk, love." He was terrified, scared that he was losing his wife. His hands shook as he ran them down her face then to the arrow protruding from her stomach. It was embedded deep in her abdomen. If he pulled it out, she would bleed to death.

"My love," she said again, "I do not…"

"Do not talk, Farah, I am begging you, save your strength." Edgar was beginning to cry. "Please, my love…" He kissed her mouth and came away with blood on his lips. "I will make everything work, I promised you."

"I know…you did…" She smiled.

He looked at her, and then behind, to find that the guard with the sword was crawling towards them. He then looked at his wife. He kissed her again and got back to his feet. Seething with anger, he walked back to the guard who tried to reach for his sword. Edgar kicked the blade away just in time and then lunged and snatched it up into his own hand. Like some demon, he looked down on the guard who was extending his arm in his defense, shielding his face from an inevitable strike.

"Please... do not," the man said.

With no mercy, Edgar swiftly brought the sword down, powered with all the anger and fear inside him, and cut the man's head clean off his shoulders. The severed head rolled down, blood gushing from the cleaved neck and remaining torso, spewing a thick stream of vital fluid at Edgar's feet. Turning slowly, menacingly, he walked to the man that had the crossbow. The guard had been mostly dazed from the punches but was still somewhat conscious.

Edgar kneeled by his side, looked at the man then raised the sword high up, holding it with the point downward. He brought it earthward into the man's stomach. The guard grunted then screamed in pain. Edgar raised it up again and brought it down into the abdomen once more. The man screamed and begged. He clutched at the blade, cutting his hands in the process.

Edgar removed the sword from the enemy's stomach, and then helped the man to his feet. He was coughing up blood all over himself and Edgar, who walked him to the tree and propped him there.

Edgar took a step back and looked at the man, feeling no pity or remorse for what he was doing to him. *It felt good. Yes, revenge was good, he had to pay*, Edgar thought as he gripped the sword handle tighter and tighter.

It was the only way for his actions to be punished. It was liberating to take matters into his own hands, to finally dispense justice his own way, the way he saw fit.

With one swift strike he impaled the man with the sword, the blade cutting through the body like paper, penetrating to the other side and lodging itself into the tree. The guard gasped for air, his arms reaching for Edgar who still stood there holding the sword.

Edgar stepped back, watched the man die, and then walked back to Farah who was now perfectly still. He checked the embedded arrow once again. There was no way he would take it out, it was far too risky. Her chest still moved slightly. She was still alive, he told himself, but was not sure for how much longer.

"I made a promise," he whispered as he scooped her up. "I made a promise, love."

He walked away with her in his arms. It was not long before he reached the creek. Farah was still unconscious, still breathing but only barely. He lowered her down and washed her hair with cool water, then cupped some of it in his hand and dripped it into her mouth.

He cleaned his own wound the best that he could, ripping parts of his shirt to make a crude bandage. There was nothing around, just the trees and the birds that still sang their song. He thought of the two guards he killed earlier and wondered who was going to find their butchered bodies. He wondered if Kenway or the Church would send more men after him and Farah. Perhaps they would give up and pay them no mind, count them as lost or killed in the wilderness. Anything was possible.

For all he knew there could be an entire search party coming after them.

"We should keep moving, love," he looked at Farah and said. He lifted her up again and continued to walk. He was tired and hungry, after what felt like an hour of trekking, he reached the edge of the forest and saw a field beyond it with several houses scattered about.

There could be someone there that could help, he told himself. He had to get the arrow out of Farah somehow, without her bleeding to death. Her life hung on a thin thread and that thread could snap at any moment. Time was not her ally, but then again, it was no one's ally. Time was everyone's worst enemy. It robs everyone blind.

Excited and with a great deal of hope, he ran with her in his arms out of the woods and onto a tiny dirty path that lead to the village. When he came out to a clearing he could see the entire town, his mood changed.

Edgar's hope immediately disappeared as the scenery below delivered a powerful blow to his psyche. The village was empty, save for all the dead bodies that were lying about. Three of the dozen homes were on fire. In the center was a giant pyre with bodies scorching in the sea of flames. Edgar was not sure if the villagers had been alive or dead when they were piled up and set alight, however they were most certainly dead now.

He placed Farah on the ground and decided to walk further down and investigate. When he reached the first house, he gagged at the putrid stench that engulfed him. The smell of rotting and charring flesh was overpowering.

In the small home Edgar discovered three corpses. Their limbs were intertwined, and they were piled on top of each other like kindling. They were fresh, it was apparent that they had died just recently. He guessed that the family was either murdered for some reason or they had died from the pestilence and were tossed aside in preparation to be set aflame. He could see that there were buboes on their bodies, puss still coming out of some of them.

Curiosity led him a bit further into the village.

However, whatever it was he was looking for, was not going to be found here. It was the village of the dead. No help for Farah, nor for the poor souls that suffered such a tragic fate.

He ran back and scooped Farah into his arms, oblivious of his own shoulder wound, and entered the forest once more. This time he decided to go the opposite way of the creek, up the stream and see if his luck changed.

Luck, he thought, was not on his side. He thought of Bradyn, his wife, Cederic...the world was cruel, and the people living in it even more so.

Hours more of walking had passed and moving upstream yielded results no different than his earlier venture into the bereft village he had discovered. The sun was beginning to set and the forest grew darker. Hunger ate at his stomach and his weakened state began to play tricks on his cognizance.

His mind turned the shadows in the woods, into terrible monsters and demons out for blood. Each time Edgar turned around to see if anyone was following them, his vision blurred and he became dizzy. Everything started to move slowly, it felt as if his limbs were dragging through molasses. Yet he became hyper aware and could hear his own breathing amplified. His heavy, labored breaths seemed painfully dragged out and each beat of his heart seemed to pound loudly in his ears and he was certain that they could be heard throughout the forest. It was if an eternity spanned between each beat.

He had lost a great deal of blood, he told himself this in an attempt to explain his state of mind and the tricks that the forest had been playing on his sanity. His extreme hunger and blood loss had contributed to his anxiety and exhaustion.

A figure, shrouded in darkness appeared some distance ahead of him, standing still in the shadows, its power drawing him, calling him toward it. He blinked and squinted, wondering if this was just a mirage, a figment of his imagination, his paranoia getting the best of him. Farah was still in his arms and he held her firmly as if someone would steal her from him. He refused to let his lover go until he was sure that she was safe.

The figure beckoned him. There were no words, no audible communication, just the mysterious aura and energy that seemed to be grabbing him with invisible hands and drawing him along.

"Hang on, love," he whispered to his wife. His words sounding distorted and strange to him, different and almost as if they were not his own. "I will not let them get you." His words scared him, showering him with a cold feeling of dread.

He looked at Farah and brushed her greasy hair from her forehead. She was cold, dead. It was too late for her.

He failed her. All the promises he made to her, he thought, ended up to be all lies. Her lifeless body hung loosely in his tired arms and that was a testament to his inadequacy, to his inability to protect what was his.

Tears began flowing, forcing themselves down his face as he started to retreat. He tried escape to anywhere else but toward the dark figure. Yet, the little voice inside his head told him to stop resisting and that fleeing was not the correct path to take. The voice urged him to go toward the spectral person standing amidst the trees summoning him.

The mysterious person extended an arm in offering of help it seemed. But after all the previous events, Edgar was unsure that this was not some sort of a trick that he would come to regret.

Edgar began to move forward, somewhat unwillingly, toward the person. His head started to spin, to ache incredibly as if his skull was going to crush itself. Weak and beaten, he dropped Farah on the ground and tried to keep himself steady before his legs suddenly gave out.

Death could not have been so prolonged and elaborate, he thought as the forest became an evil carnival in his eyes, driving him to the edge of his sanity. This was not an ordinary death. It was something much more, something incredibly, maliciously orchestrated by the forces clearly unknown to him.

He was on all fours, like a dying animal about to meet a violent end. He crawled toward Farah's body but with each movement his body ached more, resisted more, and fought back like it was an entirely separate entity.

The figure continued to beckon him to join it within the comforting darkness. Next thing he knew, the figure was upon him and he was plunged into complete darkness.

CHAPTER THIRTEEN

Francis walked through the main hallway of the church, confused, lost, and feeling as if he were stripped of his humanity. It was the unjust suffering of others that had ravaged him bare, that had shattered something he had been conditioned to believe in. The voice that had guided him to up to this point was gone. He listened for it more carefully now but it was not there. Was it ever there, he thought?

He continued past the closed doors of the rooms that the monks lived in. Francis wanted to reach out to those who could be reasoned with, those who would listen to him and see the errors that they have made. Was it righteousness that they were trying to preach and attain, or has their bloodlust simply taken over at some point? Was it ever righteousness? Was it the so called word of God? He could not tell.

All he knew was that he could no longer stand and witness as the innocent people were slaughtered. Watching them die was almost as bad as killing them himself. He might as well walk away and leave it all behind, he thought. He was too small, too weak, and too insignificant to bring about any changes in the church that was so set in its ways, that it had been holding everyone back, crippling their vision of humanity.

He made his way to the front door and was almost out when he heard someone call out to him from behind. The voice was all too familiar and it had jolted him from his thoughts. His heart skipped a beat. He turned slowly and saw Samuel standing there with hands at his chest, resting there and holding a wooden cross, the likes of the one Francis had abandoned earlier.

"Hello, Francis," Samuel said as his lips curved into a smile. "What are you doing?"

Francis hesitated as he pondered an answer. He never liked Samuel. Samuel enjoyed killing, it was apparent that he loved his duty in the dungeon, decapitating people and bathing in their blood.

"Going for a walk," Francis finally said. His answer was anything but convincing.

"Interesting," Samuel replied, obviously probing into Francis' motives and having fun doing it. "Where to?"

"Just out. I need to clear my mind, Brother Samuel. Anything wrong?"

Samuel giggled. "Oh, many things are wrong, Francis. I have been seeing things, you know, strange things that keep happening in and around this village."

It was him, Francis concluded, that had been spying on the villagers. He was the rat that reported everything back to Father Lawrence and Lord Kenway and sent so many people to their deaths. It was all too obvious now. The vermin had his eyes on Francis this whole time. There was no way of fooling him now.

"What are you talking about?" Francis asked, stalling in an attempt to come up with a plan of how to escape from the mad man.

Samuel took a step forward. "Let us be honest with each other now, Francis. There is no need to lie. I have an important job; you know that, I know you do." He took another step, a little to the side as if he was preying on Francis and trying to find the best angle of attack.

Francis shook his head, still trying to pretend he was clueless about everything.

"I was tasked with bringing the wicked, the trespassers against our faith, to justice. I was tasked to keep an eye out on anyone that would go against our church." Samuel crossed himself then continued, "I believe that I have performed my duties justly thus far."

"So what do you want from me?" Francis asked.

Samuel didn't answer.

"Well?" Francis said again, the silence and Samuel's stare was making him uncomfortable.

"Where is your cross, Brother?" Samuel finally asked and took another step forward; his arms still folded at his chest.

"I must have left it in my room," Francis answered.

"Shame," Samuel said. "I need to take you with me then, Francis." He extended his arm toward Francis, imploring him to come along.

"I am not going anywhere," Francis said sternly, with some courage even. He was surprised at his resilience for the moment.

"I will not ask you twice, Francis," Samuel informed, his smile now gone. In its place was an evil, menacing grin. "You will come with me one way or another. I have to bring you in, Francis, you see, your mind is not in the right place."

"My mind is in a perfectly right place, away from this bloodshed," Francis said with conviction and turned to walk away.

Samuel lunged at him and grabbed him by his robe, pulling him back, choking him by the collar in the process. Francis fell on top of Samuel, breaking free of his hold. He tried to get up but Samuel pulled him down again, turning him over and getting on top of him. Bony hands wrapped around Francis' throat and he began to choke. He was lucky that Samuel was not a strong man, nor a big one for that matter. With some effort, he removed Samuel's hands from his neck, as Samuel hissed like some wild, rabid animal.

As he broke free, Francis pushed the maniacal man off of him. Samuel stumbled back and hit the wall like a rag doll, knocking the shelf with burning candles on it. It all came crashing down onto his head, stunning him. Samuel shook the pain off and became even more infuriated. He jumped back onto his feet and went after Francis one last time.

Francis used the moment of freedom from the madman to grab a metal candle holder from the shelf that was situated next to the second floor stairwell. He took the candle out and turned the metal object into a bludgeoning weapon. As Samuel got closer to him, flailing his limbs like a lunatic, Francis swung the holder with both arms and hit Samuel in the side of the head. The sound of the monk's skull cracking made Francis cringe.

Blood squirted from Samuel's wound as he fell down, all his movements coming to an abrupt end as he slumped to the floor. Francis still held his weapon, gripping it tighter as he checked on his attacker.

He was not exactly sure if Samuel was dead, though there was a great deal of blood coming out of his head wound, creating a little red pool around it that was seeping into the joints of the stone floor and running like a river. He was sure, however, that Samuel would not be getting up any time soon to attack him.

The sounds of footsteps coming from all directions filled the hall and, without any further hesitation, Francis pulled the hood over his head and left. He ran as far as his legs could carry him and kept going until the church and the manor were well behind him. He finally stopped when he got right behind the hill and could no longer see the village.

For the first time in his life, Francis was presented with a wide open road and no real quest ahead of him. He looked around to see if anyone had been following and when he was reassured that he was alone, he continued his journey away from the village of Blythe's Hollow.

CHAPTER FOURTEEN

"This is madness!" Kenway yelled and threw a full mug of ale across the room. It slammed against the stone and the contents now streaked and dripped down the wall.

All the servants walked out of the room, their heads down in fear.

"Lord Kenway, please," Father Lawrence spoke softly, trying to calm the man down. "I am sure this can all be fixed easily. I am sure that many of the culprits that have posed any sort of problem are long gone."

"That is not good enough," Lord Kenway said. "What about the man and the woman that ran into the woods? No one has been able to find them!"

"I assume that they are dead," Father Lawrence said. "They have received their just punishment, I am sure of that."

"How do we know that?" Lord Kenway asked.

Father Lawrence was silent.

"Exactly," Lord Kenway said and poured himself another drink. He greedily drank it, some of the ale spilling on his beard. He burped without excuse then roughly wiped at his beard. "We have no way of really knowing. They could have very well have joined however many more escaped villagers that have been plotting against us. A village on the rise like this is not good for me, Father, nor is it good for you. When chaos ensues, there is no progress and no profit. These people need to know their place. I believe I have mentioned that to you before."

"You did," Father Lawrence said and nodded.

"How did we come to this?" Lord Kenway finally calmed down a little, his voice lower and less stern. It puzzled him how Blythe's Hollow had gotten so out of control and how the villagers were on the rise and starting to resist any authority imposed on them.

He finished his drink and poured another one then paced around the room. More of his beverage sloshed around as he moved about with agitation.

"I can have more of them brought in for questioning," Father Lawrence said. "There is always someone out there spreading lies about our good Lord up in Heaven, indulging in witchcraft, conspiring with Satan and what have you." Father Lawrence crossed himself and uttered a quick prayer. "These people need to be aware of what awful fate awaits them if they stray from our Lord's path. I am here to ensure they follow the word and that they are obedient to you as they are to me and my brothers."

Lord Kenway pondered ideas as he listened to Father Lawrence speak.

"Even if all of Blythe's Hollow needs to be brought in to confess, then that is what must be done as our Father in Heaven has bestowed that duty on us. If the entire village is filled with sinners, they must confess, every single one of them. All it takes is one bad apple to ruin the whole batch, my son."

"Well then," Lord Kenway said, as if some marvelous idea shot through his head like an arrow. "I shall have my men bring some of them in. What I need to know from you is who do we suspect the most? We are getting to the bottom of this tonight and I will kill them myself if I have to. I shall spare no one, mark my words."

"If that is your will, I will talk to my brothers at the church," Father Lawrence said as he moved towards the door. He walked out and left the man there by himself.

Lord Kenway stared at the wall while grinding his teeth. He looked at the spot where he threw the mug earlier. The streaks of his drink had traveled down the wall and collected into a pool, splatters of liquid could be seen all about the room.

He would have his village back just like it was before. He would get it at any cost. If they did not fear him before, they would now. If the ground had to be soaked in blood and new peasants brought in to populate the empty places, well then, he would raise Hell on earth to do so.

"Mary!" he yelled. "Mary!"

A woman opened the door and poked her head through. "Yes, my lord?"

"Clean this up, before we get ants all in this place," he instructed sternly and on the way out the door he slapped the woman's ass so hard that she winced. "And later," he added, "I want to see you in my room upstairs. Do you understand?"

"Yes, my lord," Mary said as she lowered her head obediently.

Lord Kenway walked outside to look for one of his most trusted guards, Harrigan. The man was lounging on the ground with three women who were Kenway's servants at the manor. They had been talking and enjoying the sunshine. The maidens immediately got to their feet and held their heads down as Kenway approached them. Harrigan, on the other hand, slowly got up and adjusted his belt with the sword strapped at his side.

"Lord," he said and the women murmured the same in unison. Kenway eyed them all individually with disgust. The young lassies made haste back to the manor to give the two men some privacy.

"Harrigan," Lord Kenway said and grabbed the man by his shoulder. "I need you to do...things for me."

"Anything, my lord," the red headed man said. His face looked like it had seen many conflicts and his scars each had a story of their own. He was missing a few teeth as well. He was battle worn and what made him so extraordinary to Kenway was the fact that he would never go down without a bloody fight.

"The priests are going to be in and around the village, looking for...troublemakers, if you know what I mean. I need you to go with them. Take a few men as well. Take the real killers, those you would fear to be up against yourself."

"You know I fear no one, my lord. I shall fight any man in Blythe's Hollow and beyond."

"And that is why I like you. But you know what I mean. Take the cold ones, those that will kill without any hesitation."

"I will, my lord, you have my word."

"Any resistance from anyone, and I mean anyone...kill them. Kill them on the spot," Lord Kenway said and walked away.

****

The man was strapped into a chair that at some point had been soaked in blood; the now dried liquid gave the chair a sinister, dark crimson color born from the countless victims that had perished in it.

His arms and legs were strapped by small leather belts that prevented any movements. A piece of stained cloth was balled up and shoved into his mouth to impede him from screaming. It was now soaked in his vomit which dripped onto his bare chest that was covered with small bleeding cuts.

The door opened and two priests, led by Father Lawrence entered. Lord Kenway walked in last, his face grim. Lawrence and Kenway came around to face the man while the other priests stayed at the door.

"I believe this is the man you were looking for?" Father Lawrence asked Lord Kenway. "He was brought to us on suspicion for conspiracy and dabbling in witchcraft." He then turned and regarded the man for a moment.

"I believe this to be him. Some of my guards saw him talking to the other man before he ran off with his wife."

The man shook his head violently; detritus of vomit flying from the cloth in his mouth.

Father Lawrence nodded and sighed. "It is a shame. One by one, they give themselves over to the Devil and look where it leads them." He stepped closer to the accused and examined his tired face. "Tell me, was any of it really worth it?"

The restrained man mumbled something incoherently until he started to gag. Father Lawrence motioned to one of the nearby priests to come and remove the cloth from the man's mouth. The priest did so and then returned to the door.

"You must believe me!" the man blurted as the gag was removed, saliva mixed with blood and regurgitate was dripping from his bottom lip and sliding down his chin. "You must! I do not know anything about him or his wife! I have only spoken two or three words to him, no more!" Tears ran down his face as he pled his case.

Father Lawrence turned to Lord Kenway and said, "I will leave you to it. I hope you find what it is you are looking for." He nodded, turned to the bound villager, blessed him and walked out with the other priests.

Lord Kenway stood by the peasant man's side and looked at the bloody wall in front of them. The room was dimly lit, as were the others, with a crude and simple torch burning on the two walls, creating stark and sinister shadows that bounced about with each feeble flicker of the torch flames.

He stood there silently as the bound man in the chair babbled nonsense that Lord Kenway was so used to hearing. Finally he tapped the detainee on the shoulder as his jabbering turned to sobs. Kenway walked around to face him once again and rolled up his sleeves. "You know," he began, "I have a talent for sniffing out liars. You know how that is?"

There was no answer.

"It is in the eyes, you see. Many people forget about the eyes and everything they hold. Oh the stories someone's eyes can tell you. Volumes and volumes of memories and gossips, even one's very thoughts can be seen from the eyes if you look close enough. They say eyes are a gateway to one's soul. I say whoever said that is damn right."

He stepped closer to the restrained peon and leaned into his face. The terrified man tried to look away but Lord Kenway grabbed his chin and held it firmly. The man's eyes frantically wandered back and forth.

"I need you to tell me everything you know," Lord Kenway whispered. His voice was menacing.

The man simply shook his head and continued to sob.

"What? What is that? Is that supposed to tell me you do not know anything, or you will not say anything?"

"Puh-please, do not…"

"I see. You just want to play dumb. It is alright."

Lord Kenway walked over to small table set against the wall; there were several kinds of tools on it. "I think you might be lying, either way, but we will get to the bottom of it, I promise you that." Lord Kenway took his time perusing the wares then returned with a hammer and a chisel and showed them to the peasant.

The man's eyes widened in horror. "Please…I beg of you, my lord…I do not know anything. I-I have no idea where he went. M-most likely to see the witch!"

"Where is she? Why can no one find here?"

"I do not know that…puh-please, you have to trust me."

"Make me trust you."

Momentary silence ensued as the trembling man pondered what to say.

"I guess this will have to work," Lord Kenway said as he approached the man and placed the chisel in his mouth. The man mumbled and gagged again as he felt the rusty taste of cold iron in his mouth. It clinked against his teeth and made him shiver. Lord Kenway raised the hammer and brought it down quickly, knocking the tooth into the back of the man's throat. He choked on it and then forcefully coughed it out along with a sizeable blood clot. He screamed and cried in agony, feeling as if the nerves in his mouth had shattered like glass.

Lord Kenway stepped away and saw that the peasant that was about to pass out from sheer pain. The blood, mixed with snot and tears, continued to run down his chin, mixing with the previous detritus. "This is in your hands, you know? All of it. I simply just want some names and the location of the horrible witch that has been a thorn in my side. I know all of you are together in this somehow, all holding each other's hands, like some silly little children."

The man continued to shake his head in denial.

"Very well then," Lord Kenway said and then placed the chisel back into his captive's mouth and hit it with the hammer once again. Another tooth broke off from the gums and got lodged under his tongue. Blood continued to fill his mouth. He managed to spit it out and as he did so, some of it flung onto Kenway's trousers.

The lord looked down and saw the red splotches covering his pant leg.

The man now muttered incoherently, his stuttering words were now just gurgling sounds of pain and desperation.

"Look what you have done!" Kenway said, anger creeping into his voice. He had been calm and collected up to this point but now he became frustrated with the lack of cooperation and with the fact that he was covered in the man's filth. "Pathetic excuse for a man!"

He roughly placed the hammer on the man's swaying head and began tapping him as if to get his attention. It was hard to tell if the prisoner was actually dying from the blood loss or if he was merely losing consciousness, yet Kenway was determined to inflict more pain and agony upon him before he departed from this world. It was how the old man worked, how he was as a person. To him, the rush of power was the greatest feeling a man could have, and he thrived on it. The power to take a life, he believed, was the greatest example of a man's might and to him that placed him in a league with God.

As he told everyone at one time or another, nothing happened in his village of Blythe's Hollow without his say so. The fact that the people were as rebellious as they had recently become, well, that was on him, he thought, and perhaps the priests too. That was unacceptable.

"You will not die until I tell you, understand?" he said slowly, his voice sounding like that of a demon, low and guttural. "As you leave us, as you wither away and die in this smelly, rotting crypt, remember that it was me who had power over your life. You could have just walked away from here had you given me someone else, someone who obviously would not care about you as much as you do about them. You are protecting who, and for what? For some petty witchcraft that is getting you all killed one by one? You all disgust me. You are all nothing but scum, insignificant little flies on a pile of shit. Little flies spreading their filth and disease." He foamed at the mouth as his anger increased and began to get out of control.

The captive's eyes rolled and then briefly made contact with Kenway's. Lord Kenway then straightened himself out and calmly placed the chisel in the middle of the man's forehead, he reared back then let loose and delivered a powerful blow to it with the hammer. The chisel tore the man's skin and cracked the skull, lodging deep and burying itself halfway into the brain.

He let go of the man's head and walked away toward the chamber's exit. As he did, the door opened and Father Lawrence came in.

"Well?" Father Lawrence asked. He regarded Kenway for a moment as he had not seen the man's face this red before. He then turned his attention on the peasant in the chair and the blood surging from his forehead like from a little fountain.

"I guess he really did not know anything," Lord Kenway said and walked by the priests and into the hallway.

"Shame, such a shame." Father Lawrence crossed himself and walked out.

****

Francis traveled along the tree line until the village was out of sight. Walking away from it felt as though he was leaving behind a large part of his life in all the madness. It felt as if his body left the Church but his spirit remained there, the two separating upon his escape.

It was just the shock of him leaving, he thought, to be so far away from the Church he grew up in. His entire life, up until this point, was mostly confined to the walls of the Church that was now being filled with blood.

He was so blind, so brainwashed from such a young age that by the time it had hit him over the head and made him realize the true pain and suffering of others, it was already too late, or so he thought.

Leaving it all behind had to be right, had to be the move he had make to clear his sanity. *But would it ever heal? Would the images of cut up, tortured villagers ever leave his mind, or will they forever linger there and torture him to the point of insanity?*

There was really no true answer he could give himself. It was all a speculation now. There was no Bible in his hand to guide him to the answer. That was what weakened him, he knew it. The book that preached so much good, yet it was nothing but a fairytale, had turned itself into a weapon.

He walked a little longer until his legs grew tired. He decided to sit down and take a break until he saw something on the ground not that far ahead. He stood there trying to make it out. Hesitantly, he started toward it and when he got a little closer, he realized that it was a body. As he approached, he saw that there were actually three bodies on top of each other.

The two women and a man that had been stacked in the pile were all dead, and by the looks of it, the deaths were recent. Francis covered his mouth in disgust as he came face to face with the disease. The bodies were naked, their clothes thrown about nearby. Each one of them had boils around their armpits that had been leaking blood and pus for some time, creating tiny pools of foulness that had soaked the ground under them. Each of the boils was the size of an apple and he winced trying to imagine the pain these poor souls had to endure.

He collapsed on the spot, his knees buckling under him, letting him fall next to the corpses. The stench had gotten to him, so he vomited whatever little was left in his stomach. Looking away from the victims was almost impossible. He had to see the horror that the pestilence had brought upon the world. Such grotesque and vile work could not be of any loving, heavenly being.

He wiped the corners of his mouth with the sleeve of his robe and crawled back away from the vomit and the bloody, contorted bodies. *Why were they here? Someone had to bring them here, perhaps in an effort to burn them. Or maybe it was an army of bandits who wanted to rob the villagers until it was discovered that they were disease ridden. Who knew? It didn't even matter anymore.*

To cross himself and bless the dead was only a brief thought that entered his mind but he quickly brushed it aside. He got up and stood there for a moment, then simply walked into the forest without saying a single word.

The dark in the woods was comforting, almost welcoming, as he started to weave in between the trees. He felt somewhat sheltered, protected from the vile light of the day outside of it.

As he meandered nowhere in particular, he thought of the times his mother told him never to go into the woods alone at night. *Evil spirits reside there, out to get the wayward little children.* He remembered her voice and words now. She had been dead for a long time, along with his father.

The same teachings continued when he decided to become a monk and when he took the vows. For as long as he had ever known, people were always discouraged away from the forest, due to the evil that lived there. He wondered why that was, wondered if that was just another lie that he was fed in his miserable life.

He stopped when he felt a little tug on his robes. It scared him and he jumped forward, when he brushed whatever was grabbing him. When he turned around, there was nothing there. Yet Francis could feel an energy moving away from him, almost pulling him along, and with that came the whisper that he could only hear in his head.

CHAPTER FIFTEEN

E dgar saw Farah in the middle of the woods, she was unaware of his presence or so he thought. She stood there amidst the trees, her hands by her side, back turned. She wore a plain white dress that he had never seen her wear before and wondered where she had gotten it.

What puzzled him more was how she had recovered from her wound and was standing there like nothing had even happened. He called out. "Farah," he gently said to her and began to walk towards his wife. She did not turn around nor acknowledge his presence. "Farah, love, are you alright?" he asked.

He continued towards her. Leaves and twigs crunched under his feet, their sound drawn out and amplified. He was feeling them, hearing them as if they cracked right next to his ears. He noticed that even the light in the forest looked strange, the atmosphere of it odd and perhaps somewhat unsettling.

"I carried you and…I must have passed out myself. How long have you been up?" he asked worriedly. Then he remembered the arrow wound on his shoulder and reached for it, but discovered that it was no longer there. Edgar felt no pain either. Again, it was as if nothing had ever happened. He remembered fighting the guards, decapitating them, their blood spraying like a fountain. Yet there was no trace of that or any other conflict on his body. It looked like the same with Farah, her gut wound was not visible.

"Farah?" he called out again. He walked a little further until he finally realized that she was moving away from him. It was not that she was walking away from him. It was as if he had been walking in place, never really approaching her. He stopped for a moment then took a few steps forward. The further he walked, the further she got away. He

97

began to panic because he could not reach her and she was not acknowledging his calls.

Edgar then broke out into a run and kept calling her name. He ran for a while, his heart was pumping faster. It was beating so hard against his rib cage he thought it would burst open. He continued to call Farah, yet his love kept escaping his reach. It seemed as though she did not want to be with him. No, it was not that, he thought. Something else was wrong here and he could not grasp it. *Why was she not turning around? Why was she not coming into his arms?*

Sweat poured down his face and lower back. It was scorching now, more so than earlier. Was it even possible for it to be this sweltering? If it got any hotter, he thought the trees would catch on fire and then he would be dead for good.

Tired and wheezing, he stopped and began to pant. Bending over, holding onto his knees, Edgar tried to catch his breath. When he got back up and looked at Farah again, she was now turned around, facing him. Her eyes were closed.

Hesitantly, he walked towards her again and he was surprised that this time it worked. She did not move away and he was able to grab her. Finally, Edgar hugged her tightly, and then started to check for her wound. The dress she was wearing, the one that he had never seen before, was perfectly white. He lifted it, examined her and discovered that there was not even a scratch on her.

"Well my love," he said with excitement, "I would say this is a miracle!" He hugged her again then kissed her. When his lips met with hers, her eyes opened and he felt a connection unlike any he had ever had with her. Her eyes were completely white and they held him captive. He tried to break away from her but was unable to do so. Some force that was coming from her held him firmly and would not let him go. Everything started to spin and shift once again.

What was once a forest was now a whirlwind of colors and objects shifting and turning into something that they were not. Strangely the couple began to move in place, yet away from where he found her. Everything moved fast, unnaturally, as if they were pulled by something. It held them both, but this time he was able to break away from her kiss.

It was loud. Sounds of wind and objects turning and breaking were overpowering his mere thoughts. "*Farah!*" he yelled from the top of his lungs as he was finally able to verbalize. "*What is going on?*"

"See through my eyes," she said calmly. He managed to hear her over the chaos around them. Everything stopped. The forest, the sounds, and the changing trees all came to an end. He found himself in the village now, in Blythe's Hollow. Farah stood right next to him; her eyes were still white and looked dead. "See for yourself, Edgar." She pointed with an outstretched arm.

He followed her finger and saw the massacre that the village was plunged into. The small, modest houses burned as guards strolled through Blythe's Hollow savagely decapitating men, women, and children in their wake. The priests followed behind the guards, Father Lawrence was leading the pack, as others trailed him. They carried crosses and bowls filled with holy water. As each villager was killed, one of the priests would sprinkle some holy water on the corpse.

Edgar felt the soft ground under his feet, and it appeared as though he was sinking. He looked down, shocked to see that his feet were covered in blood. They were submerging into red mud. He then glanced around once more only to witness the guards continue to slaughter all the innocent people of Blythe's Hollow and then the priests blessing them, absolving them of their so called sins.

Edgar stepped back in horror, his mouth open with disbelief. He tried to speak but nothing would come out. Was it due to the horror he was witnessing or was it mere inability to say anything due to his shock at the scene? He did not know. He was unsure of everything.

Not entirely knowing of what his plan was, on impulse, he ran toward the guards and tried to hit one but nothing happened. His fist went right through him as if he was not there.

"*Stop this!*" he yelled and then tried to hit another one with the same result. "Farah, what is going on?"

"They cannot see you," she said, "Or me. We are here, though we are not."

"What are you saying, love?" he asked confused and afraid. His head started to hurt again. Even her voice sounded strange, monotone, flat, without her usual vibrancy.

"We are but mere spirits in a world between the real one and a completely different plane. We can watch them, but that is all we can do."

Edgar was confused. He paused a moment to try and absorb what his wife was telling him before he responded to her. He turned to see Lord Kenway instruct the guards but he could not hear what the bastard was saying. Kenway was pointing at a little shack and when the guards obeyed, they busted down the feeble door and came back out, forcibly dragging a pregnant woman from the house. They handled her like she was an animal, yanking and jerking her back and forth, not caring that she was heavy with child. They kicked her in the back and she collapsed to the ground on her knees in front of Kenway. She looked up, her arms reaching for the man, imploring for mercy. Kenway took out his sword and impaled her in the stomach. The blade drove right through her. She fell to her side and died instantly, along with her unborn babe.

Edgar screamed now, his voice carrying. It echoed in every possible direction. He continued to scream for what it seemed like forever, until he thought his throat would bleed and he would no longer be able to speak. He paused, caught his breath, and continued to shout again.

He woke up screaming and disoriented. The place he was in looked like a hut of some sort, very crudely made. Fire burned in a little hearth not too far from the small, straw stuffed mattress he had been lying on. He was covered in sweat, and when he continued to look around to get his bearings, he saw Farah on another small straw bed across from the hearth. He tried to get up but his body did not obey.

"Farah," he called to her weakly.

"She is fine," a woman's voice said. Edgar looked in direction of the door and saw the woman that spoke come in.

"Do not worry about her, I have seen worse." She walked in and checked on Farah, then proceeded to sit by the fire and look at Edgar.

"How are you doing?" she asked. "I was worried about you. I almost thought I was not going to recover you from the dark."

"Where am I?"

"Here."

"Where is here?" Edgar asked, annoyed by the mysterious woman. "Who are you?"

"My name is Magdalene," the woman answered as she threw some herbs into the fire. The flames crackled and then made some sounds Edgar never heard before. It smelled good though, and it was rather soothing. "I have met your wife before, she had come to me for help. I was happy to meet you, though you were somewhat dead when I found you."

"Dead?" Edgar asked.

"Yes, dead. As in not alive. Your heart had stopped beating. You lost a lot of blood. Your love for her, the promise you made her, kept you going. It was something your soul was hanging on to. I was able to latch onto that and bring you back.

Edgar listened to the witch in awe. His eyes were wide open in amazement of what she was telling him and yet he still was not sure if he was dreaming or not. Then he remembered...

He hesitated, not sure exactly what he was going to say or how he should even begin saying it. Then it just simply started to flow out of him. It was as if the witch had somehow snatched it out of his mouth, or she could read his mind. "I had a dream that people in my village were being slaughtered."

"It was not a dream," Magdalene said. "Your spirit was there. Farah guided you, with my help, of course. Your spirits visited an event that happened mere hours ago. What you saw in your village, was real. It happened while you two were on another plane of reality, giving you the ability to see, to feel, but not to interact."

"They killed...them...all..." Edgar said slowly, in shock. He looked away and before closing his eyes saw all the various skulls and feathers lining the walls of the cabin. As his eyelids dropped he was again thrust into the blackness that was then populated with the bodies of innocent villagers. He saw the pregnant woman being slaughtered again and then he opened his eyes in fear and disgust.

"All I gave you is the ability to see," Magdalene said. "I can offer no comfort in this world but I can provide the tools for you to make it better." She threw more herbs into the fire. "They cast me out long ago for my interest in sorcery, in the spirits and the realm of the dead. Yes, I am the witch Magdalene that everyone has been talking about. Your people died because of their interest in me, you know that, right?"

"I do," Edgar said. "It was all for a noble cause at least, they were trying to save their loved ones." He sighed and kept looking at Farah. He could see her chest rise up and down. She was alive. The witch was telling the truth and he was so grateful for that. Then he turned his attention to the woman. She looked old at first glance, but she did not *feel* old. He could not really explain it, and he was unable to put his finger on her actual age. She had been beautiful once, he could tell that. There were traces of her beauty left behind along with some stray wrinkles and scars. Her long, gray hair hung to her hips and rested on her black dress that had been patched by many different cloths.

"Very well then," she said and fell silent. He watched her as she softly swayed back and forth, her lips moving but producing no sound.

"People are cruel," he said, somewhat under his breath but loud enough to be heard. The forest was silent in the night and the sound, no matter how low, carried like a blaze.

"They are," she said and nodded. She grabbed some weeds from a bowl next to her and tossed those into the pit. They crackled as the flames engulfed them. "More cruel than anything one could imagine. Yet they go on and blame the Devil. It is in our nature to turn against something we do not know, things we do not understand." She shook her head in disbelief.

"You have witnessed it yourself?"

"Like I said, I was cast out...for being different. It was long ago. I learned the true nature of man. I was young..."

****

As a young girl, Magdalene dabbled into things that made her parents uncomfortable, things that would send her to confession several times a week. Priests were regular visitors in their humble household as they tried to figure out what was wrong with a fifteen-year-old girl that was bound for the monastery.

They would not take her; the priests told her father, who would beat her shortly after the company left for being such an embarrassment.

"The girl is possessed," one of them had said, words that sent her frail mother crying into the night. "The Devil has entered her body and

is looking to lead her astray, away from God's path. The options are few..."

These strange things that Magdalene was accused of mainly dealt with healing powers she believed she possessed. These were channeled to her by spirits of every living thing that surrounded a person, she told those interested and dumb enough to talk to her in broad daylight. She told them that one could draw energy and spirits to come to aide those in need. But one had to be in tune with the spirit world in order to do so.

A few would come to her to seek her assistance to ward off evil or heal a sickness. These few were grateful though and spoke no word of their meetings. It did not take long for the whispering and gossip to start, however. Often she would hear murmuring as she passed by, others started to avoid her and would never look her in the eye. One day, a fellow villager was brave enough to boldly say what others were thinking. He yelled out and called her a name that she had never heard before. He called her a witch.

She became a recluse after all the verbal abuse from the villagers and the physical beatings from her father. Often she would wander the forest, spending time with nature. On her sixteenth birthday, after a day away in the woods, on her way home she came across a stranger that was traveling and who had passed through Blythe's Hollow. He appeared to be well off, most certainly not from any vicinity of the village. Perhaps he had come from a city somewhere, with his nice clothes and a bag several items of interest.

The man felt out of place there, on the side of the road, just passing through like he had said. She indulged in a conversation with him and for the first time in years she felt like she mattered. The man listened to her words with interest, nodding his head in approval, making faces to signal his surprise and intrigue. Magdalene was grateful that he did not seem put off by her odd ways. He too spoke of an affinity for the woods, nature, and the spirits. He did not cast her aside and call her names, or tell her that she was evil. He almost seemed relieved that the two had crossed paths that day. He mentioned that after their talk, he felt that his spirit guides were telling him that his journey and obligation had now been met. When he found out that it was her birthday, he reached deep within his bag and brought out an old, leather book. It appeared to be ancient, its pages worn and well used. The man, who had never told her his name, told her that the book's quest had come to an end, that it had finally found its home. He instructed Magdalene to keep it safe from the prying eyes of the others, from those who would not understand what the book was meant to be and the things that it could help her do.

He held the tome out to her and insisted that she take it to celebrate the day of her birth. She grasped it and held it to her chest as for no one to see it. But there was something there, something in the book that had come alive when she touched it. The book had some power in it, she knew that much and as she covered it with her rags to hide it from the eyes of whoever might had been looking on, she glanced around anxiously. When she was confident enough that no one was around, she turned to thank the man but he was gone. Just like he had come through the village, it was in the same manner that he disappeared.

That night she found her three friends she had helped in the past, those that still treated her with dignity. She showed them the book and watched confusion trace itself on their faces. She explained how she got it and the feeling that came with it, something luring in it.

It was here that she saw some fear creep in and replace the expression of confusion the two girls and a boy wore on their faces.

They retreated into the forest where Magdalene kept her little ritual stage hidden behind leaves and shrubs. It was the place of solace for her, a place where she was one with the nature, with the spirits, and with those powers beyond feeble human understanding.

She lit the candles around the ritual circle she had created and began skimming the thick and oily pages of the book that were scribed what appeared to be ages ago. The words were written in some strange language she was not familiar with but somehow she knew very well it was of pagan origin that had come from some Woad tribes out in the wilderness.

Magdalene found that even though the words were strange, she seemed to be able to easily read them, as if she had always been reading them. As she read aloud from the pages, a sense of uneasiness had slowly descended upon her little group that now began to cower, huddled together across from her. These odd words had summoned something from the other side and she could feel its presence; there was an entity there, among them, yet it was not one of malevolence. It had no affiliation to good nor evil and she felt that such entity could be used for either one, being able to be swayed for whatever the cause.

The ritual was cut short when several villagers, her father among them, barged in on them, sending the two girls and the boy running as if the spirits Magdalene had summoned were after them. Besides, the villagers were focused on Magdalene, as she sat there with the lit candles holding a strange book they never saw before.

She was dragged back to the village and the next morning tied to a pole outside the church where she was stripped naked and whipped as the priests' poured holy water on her in an effort to cleanse this malice.

Her mother wept as she watched her only child endure this cruel punishment that flayed the chunks of flesh off of her back. The blood poured down her spine and dripped into the mud beneath her.

After two dozen or so lashes, they left her there to sob in the rain. The late November night descended upon the village as all the lights were slowly extinguished one by one.

She hugged the pole with the last remnants of her energy that was slowly fading away. She was cold, hurt, and alone.

Sometime during the night, when the rain had stopped and clouds slowly started to disperse, letting the haunting moonlight cast itself upon the village, she lifted her head and looked upward. The moon was large and bright, sitting there in the sky like a token. For a moment, she found some solace in it, closing her eyes in its glow. Her mind raced back into the woods, trying to connect with the spirits she had summoned. She tried to recall some of the words she had spoken, butchering some of them, then repeating them again correctly.

She called to the spirits to end her life, take her away to the land of the dead, for perhaps it was there where she belonged.

Several moments passed by until she felt the same presence again, the same entity from the woods. A dark light presented itself in front of her, dancing in the moonlit glow of the mud and blood. It was a like some waves of dark energy that had formed itself before her, a dark being of some sort that had perhaps come to her rescue or to end her life.

She stared at it for a moment, entranced by the glow, by the beauty, and the power. Dazed, she fell off from the pole and into the bloody mud below. It took her a moment to realize that she had been freed. She looked up at the dark light once more, held her gaze on it until it disappeared.

She looked toward the woods beyond the village that were now nothing but a trace, merely a silhouette.

She ran toward them.

****

"And I have been alone ever since. Thankfully in their eagerness to punish me, the priests forgot about the book and I found it under a bush where nature kept it safe until my return," Magdalene said when she finished her story. "The less people you come into contact with, the better. So I have said to myself over the years. A vile bunch, we are, lower than the animals themselves."

She fell silent again as she observed Edgar's expression on his face. It was one of awe and understanding.

"You are welcome to stay awhile longer and gain your strength," Magdalene said. "Then you must be on your way. I help those who need it and those who are righteous in their hearts. You two have proved to be such people. I will grant you further assistance for your journey to wherever you need to go, to wherever your happiness may be. I was touched by your love for her. When I felt it, I too felt loved. I remembered what it was like to have such a feeling."

"She is my everything," Edgar said softly. "She is all I have to go on. I appreciate your help. Good people are hard to find these days. Deceit is around every corner, everywhere you look someone is there to make your life that much harder."

There was a moment of silence as he watched the fire dance in the middle of the hearth. The witch stared at the flames herself, getting lost in their glow. He saw its reflection in her eyes and for a moment he saw what she saw. Or were those his thoughts and visions? He was not entirely sure. There was a connection he felt with her, through Farah somehow. Whatever it was she did to them, whatever potions or herbs

106

they've inhaled, he felt like they were bound to her, that her power was coursing through his body.

He liked what he viewed in the fire through her eyes.

It was just.

It was a righteous maleficia.

He turned to her and said calmly and with conviction, "I will kill them. All of them."

She met his gaze and nodded, not in approval but in understanding.

"I want to kill them…all," he said again, and noticed his own voice change. A certain darkness clouded it. It almost made him shudder.

"Once you go down this path, there is no coming back," she said and inhaled the smoke that started to come out of the fire.

He nodded.

"You will be shunned, hunted, and will traverse the planes on both ends, seeing the suffering that never ends. You will answer the calls of those you want and will take on their suffering through whatever means. You will kill those you deem vile and evil. You will be the *necessary* evil."

He nodded again as if in a trance.

She turned to him and blew the smoke in his face.

He fell asleep again.

CHAPTER SIXTEEN

Edgar woke up outside in the woods again, sometime after his conversation with the witch. He sat there across from Magdalene who was sitting in front of a little pit that she had dug out for herself to use for her rituals and spells. There was a tiny fire burning inside, the flames barely reaching out of the top.

Magdalene was chanting and humming softly, keeping Edgar in a trance-like state. It made him aware of everything that was going on around him yet he was mostly indifferent to it. Her low hum kept him in check, clearing his mind of negative energy. The fumes coming out of the pit relaxed him, his muscles loosened, giving him the sensation that he was levitating outside his body, that his spirit had been separated from the flesh.

He looked around freely, and saw nothing but the darkness, save for the little area of light illuminating the spot he sat in with the witch. From above, it looked to him as if they were sitting in a perfect circle of light, with blackness surrounding them. He could see the straight edge of the tree line that surrounded the clearing they were about to perform her ritual in.

"I feel strange," Edgar said.

Magdalene continued to hum, ignoring his remark.

"This strange sensation...it is all over me, like...like someone, or something, is lifting me up, carrying me, almost."

Magdalene continued her spell for the next few minutes, uninterrupted, disregarding his words. She then paused, took a deep breath in without much effort, and then exhaled in Edgar's direction. Light smoke engulfed his face and loosened his body even further; it made him sway back and forth, turn his head and letting it drop from side to side, and not because of the sheer relaxation but because he felt so loose, like his limbs were detaching themselves.

He did not care.

His mind was filled with thoughts of Farah and their life before the plague. In his mind, it seemed that they were the only people in the world. Memories flashed back and forth as if his entire life was unfolding in his head, yet showing only the good parts.

There was no pain and suffering. The world was made for them and for them only, where their love flourished. They lived in the cabin they had always dreamed of, it was just the way they had envisioned it. In this home is where they raised their kids.

In the woods, Edgar continued to sway back and forth in the trance. Though in his mind, he continued living the happy life he always wanted for Farah, for himself, for their children that they never had. His spirit soared through the universe that his body knew was not real. Deep down he knew that it was all just a mirage, an illusion to mask the grim reality. Then suddenly the scenery began to darken.

Where there was once a clear sky, now loomed dark and ominous clouds. Farah was lost. There were no children and their laughter, no cabin, no garden or thriving plants. It started to rain, though it rained blood not water, and when he looked down at his feet, he began to sink just like he did when Farah had been showing the hellish vision of the village. He trudged through the bloody swamp, his vision blurring, eyes beginning to deceive him once more.

Monstrosities began to appear before him; long metal spikes protruding from the bloody ground and impaled on them were the innocent peasant villagers begging for help and for mercy. Agonizing screams filled the air; voices beckoned to his attention, called to him for help to save them from their nightmare. Edgar reached out, trying to extend his helping hand but each time he made an attempt, the body burned to ashes right before his eyes.

Somewhere in the field that was once the village of Blythe's Hollow, he saw Farah. She stood there in the same white dress she wore in his earlier vision, but this time it was stained with blood. She was crying dark tears from her lifeless eyes; they were streaking down her pale face and marring her skin. She stood there, her arms stretched out, pleading to Edgar as she cried. She sobbed and it tore Edgar to pieces to see his love butchered like that.

Anger filled his empty body that sat swaying in the circle of light in the forest, back in the reality that was his crucible.

In his vision he finally reached Farah and grabbed her with all his strength. She burned in his arms and he screamed for her. Her ashes turned to red mud as the bloody rain intensified and covered his body that had begun to sink lower into the sanguine filled swamp. Little by little he became one with the crimson muck. He gasped for air as he continued to get sucked down under its weight, he clutched at the soft substance but it simply ran through his hands, between his fingers, not letting him hold onto anything but the hope and knowledge that he was merely having another vision. However he was filled with doubt and fear and now his mind could no longer distinguish between reality and illusion.

When in his vision he was finally fully submerged under the mire, his body in the forest went into a state of shock and it began to spasm, as if it had been possessed by a demon. Magdalene broke out into a loud chant and spoke and sang words in a strange language. These sounds were alien to him. She chanted and threw her herbs into the fire that now grew bigger and bigger, the flames changing into even more vibrant colors. The smoke rose high up and wrapped around Edgar's limp body. It lifted him up like some spirit monster and with great strength it levitated him. The smoke curled around his head, seeking and getting into his mouth, ears, nose, and eyes.

The spirits that Magdalene had summoned took control of Edgar's levitating body that was now filled with the smoky herbs emanating from the fire and infused him with their own powers and wills. His wounds healed, both mental and physical, creating him anew, preserving his memories of his loved ones and all the happy times he had enjoyed. The memories of Farah, Cederic, and Bradyn stayed with him, deeply ingrained in his core, in the very fabric of his being.

Then, with a powerful jolt, there was the vengeful part. His eyes were filled with the visions of the massacre in his village, of the pestilence and the blood thirsty priests. There was Lord Kenway there too, sitting atop a pile of bodies and bones in his throne made from the human flesh of those innocents that he had struck down and annihilated in his quest.

Magdalene stopped her spell, the fire extinguished itself and his body fell to the ground. She waited there for a moment to rest until she then began to utter yet another spell. This one was brief and less elaborate. She was exhausted.

The words made Edgar rise up before the witch. He stood there, his eyes entirely black yet somehow glowing at the same time. There was now a different aura about him; he felt and looked stronger, more determined and ready to take on whatever was thrown at him.

"That was the most powerful ritual I have ever performed," Magdalene said and sighed. Edgar could see that she was tired and that the process had almost drained her entirely. "I have never actually cast this on anybody before."

"Thank you," Edgar said after a quick glance at his arms and legs.

"How do you feel?" the witch asked.

"Fine," he said simply and looked straight at her.

"You are now one with the spirits," the witch said. "They are in you, there to help, there to be used, but beware of how you use them. They will shape you as you shape them."

"All I want is to set things right"

"Revenge, is what I think you mean," she said as she slowly got back to her feet. Edgar helped her up. She could now feel the energy coursing through him.

"I guess that is the word."

"It is a long road Edgar, a treacherous one with many obstacles. Once you embark, there is no coming back. But you do as you will."

"I know the risk," he said. "I am aware that I cannot bring everyone back nor undo the atrocities committed upon so many different lives. But what I can do is avenge their deaths and let their spirits rest in peace."

"You speak the truth, Edgar, and all I can do at this point is send you with good spirits on your quest. May you change their lives the way I changed yours."

"Thank you for this," Edgar said and took her hands in his, holding them gently in thanks for all that she had done for him and his family. "I will never forget it."

"I'm sure we will meet again, Edgar. Our lives and spirits are shaped that way."

He nodded.

"If you come back," she said, "Farah will be waiting for you here. You go and forge this next part of your life."

She turned and faded away into the darkness, leaving him in the circle of light by himself. He stood there and pondered the task at hand.

He turned and walked away and as he went, dark waves of light surrounded him, twisting and weaving about him like some protective entity.

CHAPTER SEVENTEEN

Ten pyres were set up in a straight row in front of the church. Kenway placed a dozen guards, one behind each mound with two more at either end. Each guard was clasping their sword tightly, ready to strike at the first sign of trouble. All this was done to make sure that none of the captive villagers tied to the pyres could make their escape.

Lord Kenway stood next to Father Lawrence who had the Bible out and was holding it high up in the air, flailing it above his head. Some villagers, those brave enough to show their face in the night, ventured out to see this ghastly ordeal, to witness the slaughtering, the burning of their friends. Most of them came out of fear, hoping that if they make their presence known, perhaps they would postpone their own terrible fate. It was better to just show up than be dragged out, it looked better on them, they thought. Perhaps Kenway and the priests would believe such an act to be one of honesty, to show them that they have nothing to hide. But still, their fear remained and nothing was certain. Some of them held stern looks, other managed to hold their tears back.

"You see," Father Lawrence shouted like a maniac.

Everyone listened attentively, scared and unsure of what was to come.

"This is what happens when we go against God, people. This is what happens when you do not listen to His word. This is what happens when you do not listen to those that were put here in charge by Him, to guide you down the righteous path."

The frightened, bound peasants awaiting their fiery death behind the priest whimpered, some sobbed outright, not holding anything back. It slowly started to rain, the clouds now covering the full moon, tossing

Blythe's Hollow into an even more sinister scene with only the death flames to light the night.

"Those who go against His word, His message, will pay with their lives. Have you not learned that already? Has not that message sunk in yet? How long will it be before you learn to obey those who have been put here to guide you...to protect you?" Father Lawrence began to pace back and forth in front of the pyres.

The villagers looked on those who were about to burn. Standing off to the side was the man they heard stories about, the one with the hood over his head, the hulking one, the butcher. He stood there with a torch casting shadows upon his ragged and blood stained head cover.

"You must come forward with your sins, you must confess them," Father Lawrence continued. "We are here to listen and help. God never turns his back on those that are willing to accept him into their hearts. Even your death is for the greater good, for the greater cause. I am here to make sure that your souls are saved. I will guide these sinners from the prison of their bodies and the burdens of this world into a better one."

A soft murmur broke out among the present villagers, just quiet enough for Farther Lawrence not to hear what it was about.

"Do not mourn their death, my brothers and sisters, but rejoice that they have decided to go into God's arms."

"It is murder, what you are doing. That is all it is. Murder!" a man from the group said. None of the other villagers looked at him, fearing that he might be spotted. But it was too late. Father Lawrence paused his speech and pointed at the crowd, somehow singling out the man like he had some sort of light shining on him.

One of the guards, Harrigan, walked over to the crowd of villagers, followed by two other guards. Harrigan drew his sword and the first man in the crowd to stand in his way was cut down. Harrigan sliced him right across the chest, delivering a deep and fatal gash. Other villagers stepped back and Harrigan grabbed the one that had the audacity to speak out. The rest of the guards herded the others like cattle, enclosing and preventing them from leaving.

"You will all pay for this," the man shouted as Harrigan grabbed him and dragged him away from the others. "Mark my words; you will all pay for what you have done to us," he continued to shout. Harrigan kept pulling him and the man continued to resist, spitting in the guard's face. Harrigan stopped at once and immediately impaled the man, burying his sword to its hilt, spilling some blood and severing his intestines, forcing them to come out the other side of his body still wrapped around the sword. The man vomited blood on Harrigan's arm and fell down as Harrigan retrieved his sword.

"Scum," Harrigan said and kicked the dead man's head. He then pointed his drenched sword at the crowd and waved it left to right causing the pieces of guts to swing about. Laughing and taunting them he asked the other peasants, "You want some too? Is this what you want? I will cut you one by one, personally if I have to." He lowered his sword and looked at Father Lawrence and Lord Kenway. Both men nodded in approval.

"It pains me that this must happen, that we must continue our work. Yet it is something that needs to be done to purify our sad little village of Blythe's Hollow, to cleanse us of the evil that has inhabited our very souls." Father Lawrence signaled to the executioner, the large man with the hood over his head.

The man walked to the pyres with his already flaming torch. Father Lawrence crossed himself as he began to pray as the executioner lit the pyres slowly, one by one. The bound peasant villagers started to squirm in place, each one of them trying to avoid the flames that began to lick at their feet, the heat eventually blistering and melting the flesh, burning the meat. They cried out in pain, unable to endure the agony, as Father Lawrence continued to pray. The other villagers cowered, sobbed, and some of them even prayed themselves.

The damned that were tied on the pyres burned one by one, and just like that their cries for mercy stopped as they melted away then turned to ashen skeletons. The rain came down lightly but there was not enough of it to extinguish the violent blaze that raged on each one. Lightning struck through, cutting the dark sky like a knife and was then followed by deafening thunder that shot through the night, somewhere, not too far from the church.

The prayer continued as the fires burned more intensely and the silent cries of those that watched died down almost completely. Father Lawrence finally finished and crossed himself once more.

There was a moment of silence as he observed the charred bodies, then he turned and addressed the other villagers. "Remember, this is the fate of those who do not obey, those who do not listen to the righteous word." He raised the Bible up again. "Only with this book by your side will you attain salvation." Thunder cracked through the night again.

CHAPTER EIGHTEEN

The forest felt different. *He* felt different. Edgar sensed that he was now a part of it all, the cycle of the spirits, the wheel of energy, and cause and effect. He felt strong, powerful, and ready for the bloody task at hand, as he thought of all the loss and hardship he had endured.

Bradyn was gone, he was almost sure of that. The vision that Farah showed him back at the witch's cabin before he woke up the first time, told him everything. He did not see Bradyn there and that was enough to convince him that his best friend was long gone. He was dead, Edgar thought. He did not have to see it or be told, he felt that, and it was enough. That loss, knowing that Bradyn was no longer a part of his life, was just another strain of vengeful energy that was coursing through Edgar.

Cederic was now gone too, his own blood, the man that had brought him into this life. His father had given him all the world had to give. He was the man that made Edgar into the person he had become. Cederic was his mother and father at the same time, as unlikely as that was for a man, Edgar thought. He never knew his mother, who died during childbirth. From as far as he could remember, it had always been him and his father. And when Edgar met Farah, and then Cederic fell ill, he promised his father all the care he could provide and that giving up on life was not an option.

When he saw him shot down with arrows, another part of his being, the very core of his humanity, was taken away. It was a blow that crippled him.

Carrying dead Farah in his arms was what put the vengeful strain in him. It was the feeling of her lifeless body, the touch of her cold skin in the hot summer night that twisted his perception, his view on the world and the cruelty it offered. It was a powerful push on his sanity, on his meekness and the will to remain hidden.

The beast had been awoken, and emotions stirred deep within that wanted to rupture him from inside out. But the darkness in the forest comforted him, caressed him, and made him its own. It gave a comfortable home to his dark and bloody thoughts. He moved through it easily, almost silently, like a ghost, a dark representation of dozens of spirits.

The black aura glowed about him, shining dark light all around, moving its tentacles like elegant waves in a stream. The closer he approached Blythe's Hollow, the stronger the sensation had become. He could feel the pain and suffering of innocent lives. He could feel the blood being spilt, bodies dismembered, and lives extinguished. The pain that was theirs became his.

The witch did not tell him about that. It did not really matter at this point, he thought. It added to his fire, to his seething anger.

He reached the edge of the forest and stood there looking at his village. The lives that were sucked into its ground were like seeds sown by evil. It would be much to their surprise when they learn that he had come to do the reaping.

It was simple, really, he understood that now. He was the necessary evil brought forth to bring about the balance in such a wicked world.

He was the Righteous Maleficia.

CHAPTER NINETEEN

Blythe's Hollow fell into a dead silence. With the villagers dispersed, some of them taken in by the guards, things returned to normal for the night, just the way Father Lawrence and Lord Kenway wanted them to be. To have the peasants live in fear was the control the two cruel leaders longed for.

Harrigan stayed behind with another guard and a woman they had taken from the crowd before everyone left. They were out in the field behind the church, pushing her back and forth between them like a rag doll. She begged them to stop while sobbing and pleading, yet it did no good as they just laughed at her misery while playing with her as a cat does with a mouse.

"I would say we have done pretty good for tonight, have we not, Anthony?" Harrigan said.

"We sure did, boss," Anthony said.

"Now that is what I call booty worth fighting for. We are going to take our time with you sweetheart," Harrigan said and laughed like a madman. "We shall be sure to make you all sore and what not before the night is over." He yanked her by the arm and pushed her roughly to the ground. She tried to get up, still crying, but Anthony grabbed her, wrapping his arms around her waist and bringing her to her feet again.

"Please, do not do this, I am begging you," the woman said through tears, the rain of them washing her snot over her lips and down her chin. "Please," she continued to plead to them.

"Calm down, sweetheart," Harrigan slapped her across the face. "It shall be easier if you stop resisting."

"She has got some fight in her, does she not, boss?" Anthony said and giggled.

"She sure does," Harrigan replied, and then backhanded her across the face again. Blood came gushing out of her now broken nose. Her right cheek was cut from the force of the hits; some blood was now dripping from there too, washing down her face with the rain, coating it in scarlet streaks. "Nothing we cannot fix, my friend."

He slapped her yet again. Anthony let go of her and she again fell down to the ground, spitting blood and her broken teeth to the dirt.

"Now, we can start having some fun," Harrigan said as he busted out into his maniacal laughter again. He felt good, powerful, and in control. He began to unbuckle his pants but stopped when he heard something behind him. It was like a gagging sound, almost as if someone was vomiting.

"Calm down, Anthony, you will get your turn. Quit being so impatient," Harrigan said without turning around. He released his trousers down but then quickly turned around as he heard something loudly drop to the ground behind him.

He was shocked and surprised to see a strange man standing there, where Anthony had been. Anthony was now on the ground; his throat was ripped out as if some crazed animal had attacked him. A steady stream of blood was gushing out from the hole where his windpipe used to be.

The man that stood before Harrigan was one of the villagers. The guard was sure that he had seen him around before. But the villager looked different...darker somehow. There was something strange and unexplainable about him. Harrigan could see an inky light was surrounding all of his body, akin to black wavy tentacles, only they were made out of the shadowy light. It appeared to be an illusion, like some sort of sinister energy was emanating out of the man, radiating all around him like a wraith. It was black, just like the man's clothes, yet inexplicably, the light about him still glowed somehow.

"What...what is this?" Harrigan said, fear obviously creeping into his voice.

The man said nothing.

With his trousers around the ankles, Harrigan fell over in his haste and fear to get away, and he almost landed on top of the beaten woman, but she managed to crawl away from him. He reached for his sword, fumbling but finally unsheathed it and started swinging it feebly from his prone position on the ground.

"Don't come any closer, you bastard. You demon!" Harrigan yelled. He managed to pull his pants up with one hand and got back to his feet.

He swung his sword again, almost cutting the man's arm but missing it only by a little. He swung and missed yet again and was then grabbed by the man.

The rogue's hand closed tighter and tighter around Harrigan's throat, his fingers digging deeper into the flesh. Harrigan coughed and moaned, then dropped his sword. The hand squeezed tighter but Harrigan was not giving up, he was just not a man of that nature and had scars to prove it.

Harrigan delivered powerful blows to the man's ribs though these did not seem to bother his attacker at all. The man continued to squeeze, and blood started to squirt from one of the spots where he had dug one of his fingers in. Harrigan screeched painfully, and then started to gag on the blood filling his throat and mouth.

The man then finished him with one powerful tear that ripped his Adam's apple out, leaving a dark gaping hole there. He let go, and Harrigan began to wobble back and forth, his legs loose under him.

Harrigan pawed at his throat with his hands, blood seeping over them. It looked strange, almost as if was trying to prevent it from coming out of him. He tried mouthing something to his attacker who stood there but nothing came out of it; just some drowned gurgles.

The man in black remained there, watching his deserving victim drown in his own blood. He watched the pathetic display of what, to him at least, looked like a cry for help. It was not only a cry, he was begging.

Harrigan was on his knees, no longer holding his throat. His arms were stretched out, extended toward the mysterious man, whose black light of energy and spirits, glowed about him. The dark light reflected in Harrigan's eyes as he stared at it. It drew him in without haste and put a spell on him, for he could not look away. It held his gaze for some time and when Harrigan thought that he should have been dead already, he realized that it was keeping him alive, that it was holding him here, that it was had power over him, power he could not resist.

He begged it, begged the man, silently to let him go.

121

The man came closer and grabbed him by his hair. Harrigan looked into his eyes and saw the horror there. Harrigan saw who the man was, where he had come from, and his loss. Yes, the loss, it was there. He saw it. The visions played out and Harrigan understood why the man was there, he understood his mission and knew where the man would go next. More pain shot all through Harrigan's body, as if each one of his limbs was under pressure and was about to detach itself.

The man stood back and watched as Harrigan's body spread out like a star. He stared at him intensely, using all the power the spirits had bestowed upon him. The force trembled through Harrigan's body until it literally ripped him apart. His legs and arms detached and cleaved themselves from his torso in a grotesque, bloody scene.

Finally, the man and his spirits let Harrigan die.

He turned from the dismembered corpse and looked at the church not too far away from where he was standing.

He slowly walked toward it.

CHAPTER TWENTY

The church was mostly silent on the ground level save for the sound of the rain hitting the windows. It seemed peaceful, though somewhat melancholy. A candle was on each end of the main hall; it was only barely enough to keep the complete darkness at bay.

It appeared that everyone was asleep. All were exhausted from the events that had transpired earlier. One might walk in and claim it as a regular night, thinking that all the men were in their chambers. Though, beneath the main floor, in the cells of the dungeon, the night life continued; it was fueled by the blood of those that had been taken from the crowd of scared villagers. The sounds of their agonizing screams echoed and bounced off the stone walls.

Father Lawrence casually walked down the main hall of the dungeon and observed the scenery. The doors, as he had instructed, were to remain open so all the sinners could hear each other beg for mercy. They were to listen to each other confess their sins, so everyone knew what grave mistakes they had made. And so that they understood that there were other people they brought down with them by banding together.

It was the only way, Father Lawrence thought; the only way to eradicate the wicked sin.

He stopped by one of the three rooms that made up the hellish dungeon and saw two of the priests take turns whipping a man. He had been lashed for some time now, given the massive blood loss, along with all the skin and muscle that had been torn off and the remnants that still hung there. He could see bones in the places where he was flogged more severely. Part of the man's spine was now visible. He was only moments from death, and Father Lawrence was sure he had been begging.

Good...excellent, he thought as he continued his walk. *No other way but this. It had to be done if the battle was to be won, and these sinners would recoil in fear when he was finished with them. The village would cower at the mere sight of him.*

He kept walking, listening to the screams. They were the screams he wanted to hear, he reveled in their sound. He heard the screams before, many times, but these were different. These meant that the job was getting done.

He smiled.

CHAPTER TWENTY ONE

E dgar walked into the churchyard and looked at the door. He could count how many lives and souls have perished behind it. All the innocents that died and rotted and were now almost forgotten. If it continued any longer, there would be no one left to remember them.

It was quiet, but only on the surface. The painful cries were there, he could hear them through the silence, coming from deep within the church. He got brief glimpses, distorted visions of what was going on in there.

There was a guard there, however, walking toward him, yet still not seeing him. The guard had to be put there by Kenway himself and he knew that if there was one, there would be more. Edgar was not sure if they had been expecting him or something else, or maybe even a mob of villagers.

No, it could not have been the villagers. They were too broken, too beaten into the ground enough times to stand up once more against their oppressor. They would continue on living their lives in fear until they died, and new ones would come in their place to live in their own fear.

The guard stopped, finally noticing Edgar there at the door. "Hey, you!" the guard shouted. "Stop where you are! *Guards*! Guards!" he shouted and the next thing Edgar knew, there were three more behind him and another coming just around the corner. Perhaps he underestimated the priests and their sadistic ruler, Kenway. It didn't matter though, he thought. It was all coming to an end.

"Stop right there," the guard said again as he ran up to the door and pointed his sword at Edgar. He was out of breath. "Yes, right there. Now move back."

Edgar stood there not moving.

"I said move."

The guards were ready, thirsty for blood.

Edgar finally obeyed but as he stepped back, the dark energy around him became visible again, glowing its curious and powerful dark light.

"What the hell is that?" the guard in front of him demanded. "What abomination is that?" He began to shake. Edgar could see it by the quivering of the sword in his hand.

Edgar turned around and saw all the guards standing there, surrounding him. He addressed them. "All I want is one man that is in there right now," Edgar said and pointed at the church. "He is in there as we speak and he is slaughtering innocent people, calling them sinners. What was their sin? Their life? Their survival?"

The guards eyed him, mainly focused on his luminous, dark energy. Their weapons were still drawn and pointed at him.

"I just want him," Edgar continued. "Too many lives have been lost, perished. And for what? Just because someone else wills it. Is it God? Is it that man there that commands you? Walk away from this and I promise you will be spared. No one else needs to suffer or die. It is not what I want. I want him and him only. If you do this, you will walk away with your lives."

The guards were silent. Edgar could see that some of them even considered laying down their weapons and walking away from the battle.

Out of the darkness behind them came another voice, one that was stern and authoritative with a menacing tone.

"Kill him now, or I will have you all killed myself!" Lord Kenway commanded as he pointed his own sword at Edgar, from some distance of course.

Men no longer hesitated. The command given by Kenway was the nudge they needed, or perhaps required, to spring into the action. One of them took the initiative and swung at Edgar, but he dodged the attempted strike and pushed him aside. Another one came at him and then another, swinging and slashing through the air, but none of them could connect their strikes with their target. Edgar dodged one, hit him in the side and grabbed the guard's sword. He stabbed the man in the lower back and kicked him down to the ground.

He then swung the blade against one of the guards he saw in the corner of his eye and cut through the air, shearing the man's head clean off with one fell swoop. It rolled to Kenway's feet, but the body stayed there briefly, standing upright for a moment as if the head was still attached, as if the body had not realized it was gone. The blood gushed in a heavy stream, like from a fountain until the body finally collapsed. Kenway quickly moved to the side, obviously perturbed by this.

Another guard came from the back but Edgar felt his presence, turned around and almost fully dodged his attack. The guard's sword cut his shoulder open a little. Black blood trickled down his arm. The man swung again but this time Edgar was faster and impaled him right through the stomach, lifted him up and tossed him into the wall, cracking his skull when he slammed into the stone.

The last remaining guard managed to sneak up and knocked Edgar in the side of his head with the hilt of his sword. Edgar felt momentary pain stun him. It was powerful enough to knock him to the ground. He recovered quickly, shaking his head to rid himself of the pain but the guard was already there pointing his sword at his face. Lord Kenway stepped in too and lowered his sword to Edgar.

"Well I am going to sleep good tonight, knowing I will have your head as my wall décor," Lord Kenway said. "And you thought you could go up against me," he scoffed and kicked Edgar in the ribs. "What is it that you are fighting for, huh? Not much of the village is left. Your wife, Farah? She is dead, just like she should be, am I mistaken? That is her name?" He kicked him again.

It hurt, but he was a lot more tolerant to the pain tonight, Edgar thought.

"You *are* Edgar, correct? Of course you are. I know. See, I know things, Edgar. Nothing happens in Blythe's Hollow without my say so. Yes it has gone to shite, but I feel part of it was my leniency toward you people. But, not to worry, I have fixed that. It should be very different from now on."

The guard lifted Edgar to his feet and Lord Kenway lost no time to hesitation as he hit Edgar in the face, knocking him back. The guard came behind and hugged Edgar, holding him steady for Kenway.

"I will enjoy this for a while, but then in the end, I shall have you killed. I will display your body on a pole tomorrow and for days to come.

It will be placed right over there, so when I eat my breakfast, your rotting corpse will be the first thing I see in the morning."

He hit Edgar again. His head snapped back and when he looked at Kenway, his nose started to drip the black blood.

"What the…" Kenway exclaimed, confused.

"I would not count on that," Edgar said as the dark light wrapped around him again, glowing black. It extended out and knocked Kenway away, pushing him down to the ground. It drove back the guard holding Edgar too, and when Edgar turned around to face him, he looked at his own arms, his whole body, to see it wrapped in this dark energy.

He smiled at the guard and pointed at him, commanding the dark energy to wrap itself around the man. It did. It took the guard in its dark embrace and started tearing him apart, slowly and agonizingly ripping him limb by limb, piece by piece. It rendered him like a pack of wolves, blood and viscera flying everywhere. When the guard was no longer whole or even recognizable as a man, the dark force disappeared.

Kenway managed to crawl on all fours, rise, and kick Edgar in the face in the process, delivering a heavy blow, almost knocking him unconscious. When he grabbed his weapon, he stepped back and kicked Edgar in the ribs. Edgar could hear the bones snap inside. The man laughed maniacally, finally feeling the rush of power again. He kicked him again and again, Edgar now spitting the dark blood amidst the fury of blows against his body. Kenway, overcome with rage and power, kicked and kicked until he was winded and had to stop for a moment to catch his breath.

He stepped back and panted heavily.

Edgar turned and crawled in pain, moving away through blood and mud.

"It is this power, you imbecile, that drives everything around us. Do you understand that? The power that I have and no one else! Not you, not the wankers down in that dungeon…*me* and *only me*. And you think I am going to stop because some lowly peasants are not happy with the way things are run? Oh you have something else coming to you! *They* have something else coming! When I am done with you, and I will enjoy every moment of it as I tear your flesh apart, I will work on whoever is left in the morning. I will find your whore of a wife and I will have my way with her. Treat her like the whore she is. Then, after I am done with her, I will have my men fuck her for days. When she is no longer of any use…well, I will end her life myself. That is a promise."

Edgar now managed to get up and stumble a step or two toward Kenway.

Kenway raised his sword, and pointing it at Edgar again. "You dare not take another step, you…demon!"

"I will not," Edgar said as he pointed at Kenway. The dark energy exploded forth and wrapped itself around him, spreading his arms and legs apart. It kept Kenway there, like prisoner, stretched out and unable to move, much like the torture device found in the church dungeon that had been the instrument of demise for so many of the peasants.

"No, no…" Kenway kept saying. "What are you doing?"

Edgar walked over and picked up the weapon that the man dropped. He looked at it for a moment then smiled at Kenway.

"A man killed by his own sword. Ironic."

He brought the sword between Kenway's legs and moved it upward with sheer, brute and unnatural force, cutting the man in half from the bottom up. Edgar proceeded to cleave him slowly, making all the innards drop between his legs and onto the muddy ground. Kenway screamed in agonizing pain, the sound of his shrieking voice cracking though the night like thunder. All of this lasted a brief moment until his entire body went into shock, while his lips quivered.

The last thing he saw was Edgar starring at him with his black eyes.

The body split completely and as the tentacles of energy released him, each half fell over to its side into the bloody pool of guts.

Edgar dropped the sword and looked at the church again.

Not wasting any more time, he went inside.

CHAPTER TWENTY TWO

Edgar knew where the massacre was happening and he knew that it had started earlier in the night; he also knew that he might not find any survivors, a fact that angered him with each moment that passed. He walked down the main hall to the stairwell that led down into the dungeon. The path was blocked by a heavily barred wooden door bound by iron bands and studs. Not knowing his own limits just yet, or the power residing in him, he began to hit the door, pounding on it with his fists. After a few powerful, inhuman hits, it started to cave in. He continued hitting it until it part of the wood slats split and ruptured. He put his arm through it and removed the board keeping it locked. With this obstacle out of his way, he descended into Hell, or at least what felt like Hell.

More of Kenway's guards rushed out at him, trapping him on the stairwell. They swung their swords but hit nothing but the stone wall in a shower of sparks, the hits echoing through the dungeon. Edgar took them on one by one and started bashing their skulls off the wall, bones cracking on the impact. Brain matter splattering with blood flew all about with the force of the blows. Three of them came out and met this fate.

Two more of them were at the bottom of the stairs, waiting with their swords drawn. Edgar pointed at them and the men instantly became wrapped up in the tendrils of his dark energy. It ripped them both apart in the matter of seconds, painting their flesh and blood over the walls.

He descended all the way down, unencumbered now, walking amidst the unrecognizable, dismembered bodies, his footsteps making their bloody mark as he walked.

In the main dungeon hall he was met by three monks, standing there side by side. In the distance, at the end of the hall was Father Lawrence.

From where Edgar was standing, he saw that the priest was holding a Bible, blood dripping from it to the floor. It was fresh, most likely from the victims that met their end just moments before.

In his head, Edgar could still hear their screams.

The monks began to chant their prayer, their eyes closed, and their bodies swaying back and forth. They called for the help of God and his angels. They prayed like they never prayed in their life, truly believing that they would be spared, their bodies saved and untouched.

One of them took a chalice and flicked holy water from his fingers in Edgar's direction. It fell just short of him at his feet, wetting the filthy stone floor. He walked closer, and all three monks dipped their fingers in the chalice and flung the holy water, this time touching Edgar, but nothing happened.

"It is of no use, what you are doing," Edgar said calmly. "My feud is with the man standing at the end of this hall. Leave now, and I will not exact my vengeance upon you." The dark light was there, glowing dimly around Edgar. His eyes were black, much like his clothes that now dripped with rain water and blood.

"Do not listen to him brothers, kill him! Do not listen to his treachery," Father Lawrence instructed from the other end. "He is here to deceive you. See his true colors."

The monks continued to pray to no effect. Edgar pushed them aside and forged ahead toward Father Lawrence with absolute determination. As he got closer, the priest's prayer became louder. Much like the three monks, Father Lawrence called God and his angels to come to his aide, to rescue him from the demon standing before from him.

"I have come here to take your life, much like you have taken everything from me," Edgar said, his voice still calm. Every now and then, a vision of Farah, Cederic, and Bradyn shot through his head, sort of as a reminder why he was there.

"You will not succeed in this," Father Lawrence advised. "God is on my side."

Edgar stopped and looked around the bare hallway. All he saw was the blood and dismembered bodies of the guards on the other end and the praying monks in the middle. He smirked at their folly, at their blindness. Their God was not there and his revenge felt sweeter, more complete.

"There is nothing here, certainly no God to save you," Edgar said and then grabbed Father Lawrence by his throat. He placed his other hand on his forehead. "And now you will pay for everything you have done, all the lives you have taken."

"Oh dear God in Heaven," Father Lawrence said before his speech froze and then he started to babble like an infant.

Dark visions of torture and killings played out in his mind, all involving him and the members of his church. He saw himself and his congregation burning. He relived the guards and priests decapitating, skinning, and impaling the villagers. He saw Blythe's Hollow on fire, bodies scattered in bloody mud as he walked with Kenway and his guards.

"I am giving you some of their pain, you bastard," Edgar said. He held onto his head, transferring the pain of the innocent, extinguished lives onto the priest.

Father Lawrence went into a spasm, his body jerking uncontrollably. He foamed at the corner of his mouth and it slowly turned red as blood started dripping over his bottom lip.

This came to an abrupt stop as one of the monks came up behind Edgar and impaled him with a sword. Edgar, in pain, suddenly let go of Father Lawrence, who upon release vomited blood.

"You demon!" the monk exclaimed as he watched Edgar on the ground, the sword still sticking out of him. The other two monks came rushing to Father Lawrence, lifting him up. The man was weak, barely able to stand on his feet. He vomited again and the monks let him fall down.

"What have you done?" one of them asked as he crouched down to remove the sword from Edgar's back. "You heathen! What have you done?" the man demanded. The other two stood there and began to pray again.

They prayed and poured holy water on Edgar. The bloody Bible stood at their feet. One of them grabbed it and began sifting through the pages, trying to find a specific passage.

"You will pay for this," the one with the sword said. He held it nervously, obviously with no experience in the battlefield. "You have killed a servant of God, you demon."

"He is not dead," Edgar said as he tried to get up, but was kicked back down by the monk.

The monks looked at Father Lawrence who was still breathing in the corner there, but only barely.

"I *will* kill him," Edgar said. "So if you do not kill me right now, I will kill you in the most brutal ways your feeble minds can even begin to imagine."

Right as he said that, he heard footsteps coming down the hall, the monks paying no attention to it. From where they were standing, he could not see whose footsteps they were.

One of the monks fell down after being hit in the head, dropping his bloody Bible as he collapsed. The other monk was hit too, and the third was pushed down. The man, Edgar still could not see who he was, got on top of the third monk and began beating him with his wooden club. When he was done with that one, he went to finish the next one, then the last one.

Panting, trying to catch his breath, the man turned to face Edgar who was just starting to get back up. The man was covered in monks' blood.

"I knew something was pulling me to come back one last time," Francis, now the former priest, said as he dropped the club down. "I knew I had some unfinished business."

"Thank you," Edgar said. "I have seen you before, in the village."

"Francis," he said. "My name is Francis, and yes, I used to be a priest here. Seems like a life time ago, though my decision was only made days before to remove myself from these fiends." He looked at Father Lawrence then back at Edgar. He saw him looking at the half dead priest. "He was one of them," Francis pointed at the old man. "The one man, among many, that made me question everything I was brought up to believe in. Yet, I should thank him now for all the wrong he had shown me and opened my eyes to the error of my ways, the ways of the Church."

Edgar was silent. The dark glow was still there around him. Francis was studying him, as it as it danced in the air.

"I see that I am behind here on some events that have transpired. As I also see, you have some unfinished business with Father Lawrence, yes?" Francis asked.

Edgar did not answer. He stood there and stared at the man that caused him so much grief.

"You have taken a turn in your life that I have no place in telling you how it should end, my friend. We carve our own paths, each action having a cause and effect. I have learned that. Well, seems like I have always known that, but…you know. Anyways, do what you will. We all have our stories to tell."

Edgar looked at his arms and the dim glow. "I am too far in mine to go back, although I wish I could. Too many wrong things happened at the wrong time and this, if you will trust me, is the one and only solution," Edgar said and looked at him with his black eyes. "A man must do what a man must do to be able to exact his vengeance on those who have wronged him."

Francis nodded.

"These men took everything from me," Edgar said.

"I will not stop you from doing what you think is right," Francis said. "I cannot explain why I came back. Perhaps it was to witness this, to get closure on everything, or even satisfy my own thirst for revenge, for those that have been wrong. The moment I left the church, something was dragging me to come back. And this could have been it. There is something out there that pulls the strings, but it is not as sinister as these men have made everyone believe."

"A higher power, yes," Edgar said. "Not the God these men made up to frighten everyone with."

Edgar walked over to Father Lawrence and kneeled by his side. He placed his hand over the man's forehead again. Father Lawrence began to smoke, and eventually he caught on fire, first his clothes and then his skin.

"For everything," Edgar said calmly and removed his hand from the priest's head. He got up and watched the man's skin bubble and blister then peel off by the licking flames.

Francis watched too, without any remorse. Something inside was now whole and he finally felt at peace again.

CHAPTER TWENTY THREE

Edgar sat in the field behind the church and watched the skies clear through the night and give way to a beautiful sunrise. He felt as one with nature and its spirits and forces. The bloodshed that happened mere hours ago were in the past, as if it had happened in a different time, in a different universe.

Francis came up to him at one point, before venturing elsewhere, to wish him good luck on whatever path his life led him on.

"Thank you for coming back, once again," Edgar said and shook the man's hand.

"Like I said, thank your spirits that you have…wrapped all around you," Francis said comically, with a smile and waved his hand over Edgar where the dark light glowed earlier. "Yes, you know what I mean."

Edgar smiled.

"We must lead our own lives…"

"Edgar," Edgar said, realizing he never introduced himself.

"Yes, Edgar, that is what we must do, without some fear that lurks from above or below."

"That is the folly of man," Edgar said as he looked out at the rising sun. Who knew the sun would come out so clearly with nothing obstructing its warm rays? "That is what we are about, as human beings, always needing some drive, some reason why we should perform good deeds…"

"Or evil ones, for that matter," Francis finished.

"Yes," Edgar said. "We have created the God to motivate ourselves to do good and at the same time scare ourselves of eternal punishment by the same good. Then we made the Devil too."

"And it is all man and its construct. It is a sad world we live in, my friend. Dark, bleak…violent. But who knows, perhaps in some years, the mankind will change, for the better. We can only hope."

"Highly doubtful," Edgar said and sighed. "See how it is today, it is very hard to envision a brighter tomorrow. But as you said…we can only hope, I suppose."

Francis looked at him, wondering what to say to that. There was nothing. Deep down he knew.

The men fell silent for a moment as the sun got up in the horizon. Then Francis patted Edgar on the back and left without saying a single word. Silence was enough; the unspoken words were the ones that meant the most.

They went in different directions knowing that their lives led them to where they were at that point in time and that it was their decisions that gave the result they wanted in the end.

Francis walked past the church, the place he spent last seven years of his life. He devoted himself to a cause that had blinded him, that had made him stand on the side and watch as so many innocent lives perished right before him.

It was all over now as he had embarked on a new path.

Edgar left the village shortly thereafter and walked into the woods. Before moving past the tree line, he glanced at the village of Blythe's Hollow once more. The sun was continuing its rise slowly now and what villagers were left began to come out of their houses, one by one like little ants, just going through the motions of their lives they thought so predetermined.

Perhaps when they found the corpses of Father Lawrence and Lord Kenway, would everything become clearer to them.

He went to the place where Magdalene performed her ritual on him. She promised that Farah was going to be waiting for him if he stayed alive after his quest. He inhaled the crisp morning air, and felt very much alive, there was no other way of describing it.

He smiled as he approached the clearing where Magdalene said Farah would be. He saw her standing there, in the white dress from his visions, but this time, it was perfectly white. There was not any blood on it. The witch had made good on her promise, much like she did on everything else. She did not have to help; he knew that going into the bloodshed and giving himself over to the powers that he now commanded.

"I have been waiting for you, love," Farah said and wrapped her arms around him as she kissed his lips.

"You do not have to wait anymore," Edgar said and kissed her back.

"This means we will be together now?"

"I promise."

He had said enough and it was all she wanted to hear.

She smiled.

He took her hand in his and kissed it.

They turned and started their journey away from the clearing and as they walked, the dark light glowed around both of them.

EPILOGUE

Late autumn

The leaves have already fallen to the ground. They are dead, their color faded, spilling into the damp ground beneath them. They died just for the time being until new life comes forth again in a few short months. But much like everything in that time, that short duration could might as well be an eternity.

The clouds cover the sky in their dark blanket, casting an ominous shadow on the town that looks like it is going to eat itself in the most brutal agony. The people have turned against each other in evil ways. They are at one another's throats, tearing at each other's poisonous flesh.

Their bodies are covered in buboes, the pestilence is ever present, taking each life in grotesque ways, claiming it as its own, rotting it beyond recognition.

There are priests there too, a group of them actually. They carry a giant cross and the priest at the head of the congregation is carrying the Bible in his pale, bony hands. In the other hand he carries a whip. Ahead of them, held by two priests at length, is a man. He is naked and chained. Cuts and gashes are all over his body where the whip had made contact mere moments before. The wounds are fresh, still oozing with blood and pus.

The priests yell at the people looking on, at those fighting one another, urging those to change side with their church to remove the sinners from their life, from their town. They urge them to remove the poison and accept God's punishment, to accept the pestilence, the Black Death.

They tell them it is because they have sinned. They tell them it is God's test and they must do their best to get to the Gates of Heaven.

Everyone then stops because something strange happens, something that they have never seen before. The priests stop moving and the chained, naked man finally falls down into the mud.

A man and a woman walk through the town passing amongst the crowd of people who are in awe by what they see. They make way for them and let them through.

The strange man and the woman appear to have a dark aura around them, a black light that dances around like spirits, a dark energy. They walk through the crowd and take the ones who were oppressing the weak. They touch them, hold them and their bodies disintegrate in violent flames.

The priests are at a loss for words and the one leading the congregation starts flipping through the pages of his Bible, trying to find the right passage. He stumbles upon a page and begins to read it.

Nothing happens.

The man and the woman make their way to the priests. The men of God step back, save for the one reading from the Bible. The man grabs him by the throat and lifts him as if he did not weigh much. He chokes him until blood pours from his mouth and then the body catches on fire. The woman is on the ground, helping the naked man, removing the chains from his arms and neck. He is barely alive, but the woman knows he is going to make it.

The man walks toward the priests that had been backing away but are now bowing down.

They all release their burden. The cross hits the ground but makes no sound.

ABOUT THE AUTHOR

Emir Skalonja is a writer and indie filmmaker. He is the author of the horror short story collection Lucifer and All His Disciples. He lives with his wife Nicole and their two dogs Spike and Noa and two cats Scruffy and T.J. in Buffalo, New York. You can follow Emir on Facebook at
www.facebook.com/Emir-Skalonja-Filmmaker-Author.
and on his film production page at
www.facebook.com/foxtrotprod.

ALSO FROM OPTIMUS MAXIMUS PUBLISHING

10.35 AM, September 14th 2015. Portsmouth, England.

A global particle physics experiment releases a pulse of unknown energy with catastrophic results. The sanctity of the grave has been sundered and a million graveyards expel their tenants from eternal slumber.

The world is unaware of the impending apocalypse, Governments crumble and armies are scattered to the wind under the onslaught of the dead.

Kurt Taylor, a self-employed plumber, witnesses the start of the horrifying outbreak. Desperate to reach his family before they fall victim to the ever growing horde of shambling corruption, he flees the scene.

In a society with few guns, how can people hope to survive the endless waves of zombies that seek to consume every living thing? With ingenuity, planning and everyday materials, the group forge their way and strike back at the Hellspawn legions.

Rescues are mounted, but not all survivors are benevolent, the evil that is in all men has been given free rein in this new, dead world. With both the living and dead to contend with, the Taylor family's battle for survival is just beginning.

Book 1 in the Hellspawn series.

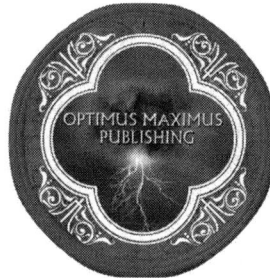

BALLYMOOR, IRELAND, 1891

Patrick Conroy, a young American student of medicine in Dublin, decides to take a break from the hustle and bustle of the big city and spend a month in the quietude of the wild and beautiful Glencree valley, County Wicklow. However, surrounded by local legends and myths, he is soon dragged into an ancient mystery that has haunted the village of Ballymoor for centuries. Set on the background of the tumultuous years preceding the War of Independence, and colored by Irish folklore, the Haunter of the Moor is a ghost story written in the style of Victorian Gothic novels.

OPTIMUS MAXIMUS
PUBLISHING

Made in the USA
Middletown, DE
05 March 2017